Snows Rest
A Maryland Mystery
Illustrated
Enlarged Print

By

Linda A. Stewart

ISBN-13:
978-0692799789 (Linda A Stewart)

ISBN-10:
0692799788

Author's Note

This is a work of fiction. Names, characters, places, and incidents are either the product of the author's imagination or are used fictitiously. Any resemblance to actual persons, living or dead, events, business establishments, or locales is entirely coincidental.

Thank you to my friends and family who encouraged me to follow my dream of writing.

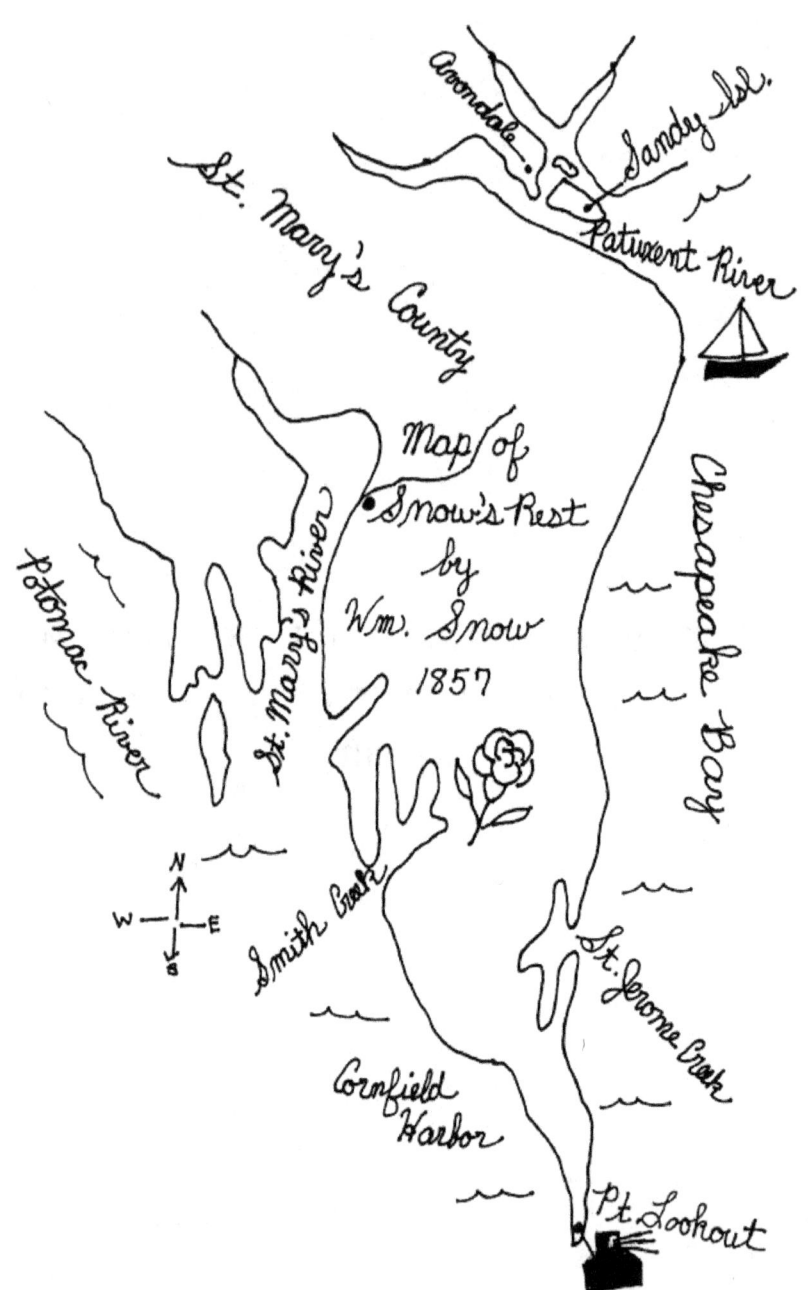

Avondale

Sandy Isl.

St. Mary's County

Patuxent River

Map of
Snow's Rest
by
Wm. Snow
1857

Chesapeake Bay

Potomac River

St. Mary's River

N
W — E
S

Smith Creek

St. Jerome Creek

Cornfield
Harbor

Pt. Lookout

2

Snows Rest, A Maryland Mystery

Chapter 1 Return Tide

Too late! Though flowerets round me blow,
And clearing skies shine bright and fair,
Their genial warmth avails not now—
Thou art not here the beam to share.
Richard Harris Barham, 1788-1845

Lifted by gentle swells, the steamship rose and fell. Water gurgled along her surging hull. Debris scraped down her port side, clawing for entry like truth demanding a hearing. During the night, a shifting return tide hastened the steamer's descent down the Bay. At Fair Haven and Plum Point, the Anne Arundel delayed her departure to adjust the schedule, before steaming down the Chesapeake surging towards Solomons Island.

William Thomas Snow sat poised in darkness. Dawn advanced under the stateroom door.   Night receded into corners, crept under the disheveled bed, and slipped behind the washstand. Stenciled roses flowered on white paneled walls. Snow remembered Jane's tea roses blooming with delicate fragrance at Snows Rest. Now they surrounded her, waiting for her skilled attention. He promised to tend them himself.

The bulbous shape of a water pitcher emerged into soft light. The Weems Line W, on a red ball in a blue field, materialized on the gleaming white ceramic background. The pitcher sat in a bowl on the washstand. Snow rose stiffly and laid out shaving mug, brush, razor, and towel. The razor slid over his silver stubble as his mind wandered. Details of the carriage ride to the docks faded, but he recalled boarding the Anne Arundel. Jane Cawsin Snow enjoyed these first class staterooms with brass bedsteads and marbled washstands. He slept poorly without her.

Snow found himself standing ready by the door and felt for the letter inside his jacket pocket. While he stood staring at the stenciled roses, the steamer corrected a few degrees to starboard on her approach Cove Point. Morning light glittered under the door and sparkled through the clear crystal doorknob. His grasp smothered the light in the cool glass long enough to feel the knob warm. He turned the knob and stepped blinking into the day.

The unusually dry, clear June morning awaiting him was likely to become a stifling, humid afternoon. Passengers bustled by in cheerful, hurried activity. Snow froze, aware of her presence. A passenger moved across the deck in the corner of his eye. Her soft swept up hair, narrow waist, and graceful walk pulled at him. The walk might be the same or the hair, but she would always be someone else. Check the impulse to look, he turned into the steamer's salon.

The high, white ribbed ceiling glistened above dark paneled walls. A rich coffee aroma sharpened Snow's appetite. He became aware of someone speaking, as a young uniformed officer stepped towards him.

"Judge Snow, Judge Snow, Captain Gourley would like you to join him for breakfast in his cabin." A feeling of familiarity lingered between them as Snow followed the purser to the captain's cabin.

Snow failed to call on Commodore-Captain James Gourley, a longtime friend, when boarding the night before. Now James said something solemn to him. Snow listened to his own jovial greeting. Gourley's first surprise turned to a knowing expression. Breakfast arrived and Snow ate as he had eaten little the day before. The two friends consumed eggs over easy, smoked country sausage in creamed sage sauce, and beaten biscuits.

Crisfield tomatoes, peeled, fried in bacon, and stewed in a black iron pan, were the finest dish of the meal. He could not get enough of the coffee. Gourley called the brew Maxwell House, named for a Nashville hotel.

They talked about the strange, cool weather. They discussed the need for an ice-free port to ship Western Maryland's coal year round. They weighed the possibility of building a railroad all the way to Solomons Island from Baltimore. They analyzed speculation the new Maryland & Pennsylvania Railroad might buy the Weems Line. The railroad bought two other steamship lines in the Tidewater Area this year. James assured Snow the Weems family would never sell the line that carried its name on the Chesapeake since 1817. Worry lurked in the strength of James' assurances. The new owner, a son-in-law, might not feel such loyalty. In this new century, change came as relentless as the tide. What had always been might soon be gone. Conversation lagged. The screw drive disengaged, leaving the hull drifting ever slower toward the dock. Gourley placed a hand on Snow's arm.

"Will, I am so sorry. It is difficult seeing you without Jane. On such a beautiful day, when you are going home to Snows Rest, she should be here, but she's not. When Molly passed away, I had a difficult.... Give yourself time. Give yourself a year, and don't be a stranger."

Snow sighed. "Yes, she should be here...and sometimes she is. She appears across a street or in a crowd. When I look, she's an imposter. I have stopped looking, but it's a shock. I appreciate the earnestness of people who believe they have seen ghosts." Snow's confided grief tumbled out like water pouring into a glass. The old friends examined their coffee.

Focused on his coffee, Gourley

confided, "After Molly died, sometimes I heard her footsteps coming up the stairs at night. It's good you're going home. You'll need time and rest."

Snow wasn't going home yet. He told Gourley about the funeral, the other funeral, the real reason for his layover at Solomons Island. When they parted, James presented him with several cigars from his private Havana stock, and promised to send a box to Snows Rest.

Back on the deck, Snow searched for a dockhand to take his trunk to the Overzee Inn. Told the purser sent the trunk ahead, Snow wanted to thank him, but the young officer had gone ashore.

Instead of taking one of the water taxis, Snow walked. He wandered the tree-lined, oyster shell paths and examined changes to Solomons Island, one of the stops on the Patuxent River Route. A lovely inn, Seven Gables, sat across the river in St. Mary's County. It was comfortable and far away from the smell of commercial canning on the island. Snow always stayed at the Overzee Inn. Two of Jane's relatives, Beatrice and Gladys Overzee, owned the inn. Family loyalty required he stay there.

Snow remembered the two women as "The Sisters". Gladys Hope married Beatrice Marie Overzee's younger brother, John Overzee. One January day, John went tonging for oysters in the company of a bottle of Caldwell's rum and drowned. Left without support, the two women moved in with a grandmother and renovated her old farmhouse to create the inn.

Together, the Sisters held an expansive oral memory of island tradition handed down from relations, neighbors, and guests. They enhanced this knowledge with astute observations of human nature developed from watching their relations, neighbors, and guests.

Postponing his arrival at the inn, Snow examined dust on his shoes and listened to the crunch of oyster shells underfoot. He avoided stepping in a cow pie. The common pasture gave way to development long ago, but some Islanders still kept a family cow. A few of these wandered at will. Snow mopped his brow, folded his jacket over his, arm, and rolled up his sleeves. Waters of Back Creek dappled in sunlight as they ran by Molly's Leg, a small island amid the current. Changes seemed to spring up like toadstools after a summer night's rain. The past, present, and future sprawled before him crowding the island across to the opposite shore.

He searched for signs of the former Sandy Island he drew on maps in his schooldays. Before the war, this was a sparsely populated fishing village. In 1865 Isaac Solomon bought most of the land and began a booming business with his new canning method. Along with building the plant, Solomon leased bugeyes and skipjacks to local watermen. Sandy Island became Solomons Island.

Benjamin Thomas Coode moved his boatyard here from St. Mary's County to build workboats for Isaac Solomon. His wealth grew, and he married Jane's cousin, Eleanor Mae Cawsin. Later, he moved his family to Avondale, across the tidal creek. He expanded his business and built a spacious home. Around the house, he planted the largest elm saplings available. The Victorian style dwelling dwarfed the trees for many years. Still, he gave the house a grand title, The Elms. This subjected him to the humor of neighbors behind his back. Now, the graceful elms swayed above the house, and the last century gave way to the new. Benjamin's title no longer evoked humor.

Behind Solomon's oyster and crab packing plant, skipjacks returned early with a day's haul of crabs. Lowering booms and tying up sails, they drifted toward the canning docks. Soon the harbor would be a forest of masts. Hammers echoed from construction at Ship Point and Avondale, two communities spawned on the mainland. Each year Avondale grew closer. The oyster-packing houses dumped shells into the tidal creek. You could almost walk across at low tide in summer.

As Snow's glance swept past the inn toward Avondale, a figure in Weems Line uniform ambled toward him. The Anne Arundel's purser came along the path with a slight limp. This time, Snow recognized him. Thomas Alexius Coode, younger brother of Ellen Mae Coode, left after some difficulty and went into the army. He joined the cavalry and fought at Kettle Hill in the Battle for San Juan. Now, he was a local hero with the difficulty in the past. Thomas addressed Snow. "Welcome to Solomons Island, Judge. We are all pleased you could come to Ellen Mae's funeral. Can we do anything to make your stay more comfortable?"

An image of Jane stepped out of the Overzee Inn. Immobilized, Snow's breath ceased for several seconds. He struggled against a vision of Jane waiting at the inn and forced himself to look away.

"Thank you, Thomas, for delivering my trunk. My Jane would want me to stay with the Sisters." Snow reached out, shook Thomas' hand, and glanced back at the porch. Instead of vanishing, the apparition raised her hand to shade her eyes and searched up and down the road.

Thomas nodded. "Of course. I take a room at the Overzee myself whenever I layover at Solomons. I am staying there now."

As they spoke, the apparition stepped down from the porch and walked toward them. Closer, Snow saw she was taller than his Jane and her walk more assertive but less graceful. She wore an indigo blue, cotton jacket with wide lapels and large pleated sleeves. The bodice flared below a narrow waist like a jacket his wife wore long ago. Closer, he saw she wore a black rimmed, oval mourning brooch, pinned above an embroidered handkerchief. A touch of Weems Line red in the embroidery stood out in contrast to the blue and white. Well pressed and neat, her apparel was still faded and out of fashion. Snow remembered Hattie Wells as the personal secretary who accompanied Ellen Mae on visits to Baltimore. Hattie's likeness to his own Jane never struck him before. He tipped his summer straw hat as they greeted each other. A letter fell from his jacket pocket to settle on the ground between them. Thomas retrieved it for him.

Towering protectively over Hattie, Thomas offered his arm to her, and she smiled as she took it. The texture of brittle, yellowed envelope in his hand filled

Snow's mind with a returning tide of memories.

Snows Rest, A Maryland Mystery

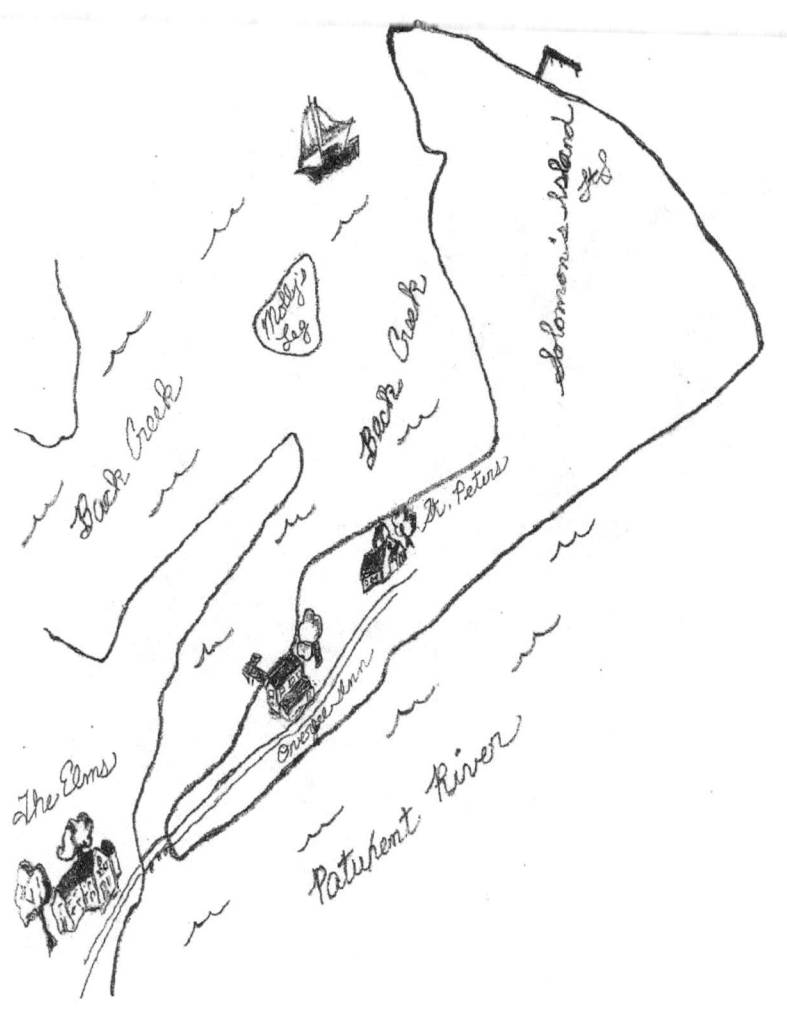

Chapter 2: The Funeral

Remember me when I am gone away,
Gone far away into the silent land;
Christina Georgiana Rossetti,
1830 – 1894

Ushered into the Overzee Inn by Thomas, Snow and Hattie paused in the front room. Down the hall, they could view the dining room. Unaware of their guests' arrival, the Sisters Overzee were in disagreement.

Absorbed in opposition over clearing breakfast, the Sisters took no notice of their guests. Beatrice leisurely rolled the last napkin, placing it in a napkin ring, tight and exact. She precisely aligned each napkin on the sideboard next to its personal saltcellar.

With a clattering of dishes, Gladys sailed imperiously out of the dining room scolding. "Beatrice, you need to crumb the cloth. It's the least you can do after I cooked breakfast and washed dishes."

"Well, I don't know as I'll do that." Beatrice retorted raising her voice and elevating her short, stout stature on tiptoe. "I have served breakfast, lunch, and supper for three days all by myself, crumbing and all. I still have the front room to clean. For once, you could..." But, Gladys was gone. Beatrice whisked the small wire basket over the tablecloth picking up breakfast crumbs. With a smile of satisfaction, she dumped crumbs on the kitchen floor just inside the doorframe. Snow's smile spread all the way to his shoes. Beatrice looked around at Hattie's giggle.

"Oh, dearest William, you're finally here." Beatrice gushed as she sailed into the front room trapping Snow in her pudgy embrace. "We have saved Jane's favorite room for you. Thomas usually takes it, but he didn't mind letting you have it. He took your trunk straight up. Now, you need some cold refreshment from our icebox. You settle yourself here in the front room, and Gladys will bring you some lemonade. We have so much to talk about."

Hattie dropped Thomas' arm and stepped toward the stairs. Failing to discern her look of alarm, Thomas reached out and took her by the elbow. He did grasp the meaning of Beatrice's nod toward the entrance and excused himself to escort Hattie home.

Snow smiled, sighed, and mentioned last night's difficulty sleeping in a steamboat stateroom. He thanked Beatrice and went up to his room for a nap. Invitations to the Overzee Inn's front room were avoided when lying over at Solomons.

Snow found his usual room at the end of the hall. It had windows on both sides, with views of the Patuxent River and Back Creek. Hand tatted and much-mended lace curtains stirred slightly. Cool breezes wafted through the room. White oaks surrounded the Overzee, creating a shaded sanctuary from summer's heat. Even after Snow closed the door, air moved through the room and over the two single beds. New to the room, a handsome rosewood mantle clock ticked away the time. One faded rose patterned quilt was turned down. The other matching quilt was still made up. With his brushed clothes hung on the valet, he settled into the cool, smooth sheets. He lay staring at the other empty, single bed. The quilt spread smoothly under the bolster. After a few sleepless minutes, Snow rose and tenderly turned down the other quilt. Back in his own bed, he drifted into shallow sleep, into a dream melding past and present.

A rosewood, six-column mantel clock strikes the hour. A door clicks open. An aperture opens in the dream. His beloved Jane walks through in her indigo blue, linen wedding suit. Someone floats behind her. A whispered exchange fades from hearing.

Light, shafting through lace-covered windows, fades. Roses bloom across the aperture and cover the door as it clicks shut. Footfalls trail away. Other doors shut distantly. Time shifts back to the Cawsin Farm front parlor. With hoops and crinolines swaying, his mother, Anna Maud Snow, sweeps into his dream. Her shy younger son, William, follows in tow. Jane Louisa Cawsin and her sister, Ellen Frances Cawsin, curtsey. Jane, William Thomas Snow's great love, admires his Union Army, second lieutenant frock coat. Ellen, red and white Confederate ribbons in her hair, looks away. Addie, Ellen's maid, sets the tea tray on the table and slips an envelope under Snow's plate. 'David' is scrawled on the envelope. This is the letter to his brother from Ellen, the letter David will read too late. Raised voices from below stairs in the Oversee Inn intrude into his dream. Snow wakes to thoughts of his older brother, David.

A glass of lemonade rested on the bedside table. Condensation dripped down its side onto a tea towel. The inside window shutters were drawn to block light. Someone had smoothed up the rose pattern quilt on the opposite bed. He rose and sponged off at the wash stand. Then he changed his collar, dressed, and went down to a funeral.

They arrived early at St. Peter's Chapel. Snow and the Sisters sat in silence before Ellen Mae Coode Abbott's closed coffin. An organist began soft funeral hymns. Members of the congregation gradually entered in muffled conversation.

Snow searched his memory for names and relationships of family members who were ushered to front pews. Some of Jane's relatives were unfamiliar to Snow. Each summer, heat drove him down from Baltimore to the cooling breezes of Snows Rest. Jane preceded him by a week or two in order to 'open up the Rest' as she put it.

She used the time to visit her Solomon's Island family alone.

Pale and shadow-eyed, an exceptionally tall man in his thirties progressed towards the front pews. Snow remembered Richard Darberry, Ellen Mae's cousin. Richard had escorted Ellen Mae to Jane Cawsin Snow's funeral. Ellen Mae's husband, James Abbott, had not attended. With a formal top hat held in his right hand, Richard guided an older woman on his left arm. Her mourning dress was grayed with time and use. The pair looked neither left nor right at other parishioners. As they stepped into the pew, she brushed lint from his sleeve, and he took her white-gloved hand in his.

A whisper stirred through parishioners like an unexpected breeze in the heat of summer. Dressed in his cavalry uniform, Thomas moved quickly down the aisle with Hattie on his arm. He stared straight ahead, his eyes fixed on the coffin. They sat in front of Richard and the woman Snow assumed to be Richard's mother.

Another couple progressed toward the front. The man guided the woman with his hand on her back. Occasionally pausing at a pew, he whispered quietly with selected parishioners. No one addressed the woman. A lanky adolescent followed several steps behind looking down or away. The three mourners sat in front of Thomas and Hattie. Snow studied this husband of Ellen Mae who had not come to Jane's funeral. James Lathemore Abbott was a businessman, business-like even now. Snow checked his urge toward resentment.

An Episcopal priest proceeded down the center aisle. The phrase, 'I am the resurrection and the life...' brought the parishioners to their feet. Mechanically, Snow continued to sing softly throughout Rite One. When the congregation sang, "Why art thou so full of heaviness, O my soul? And why art thou so disquieted within me..." the hymn settled over him like a shadow. Recollections of Jane twirled through Snow's mind, a kaleidoscope of grief. As the service progressed, air dissipated from the nave. Snow gripped the pew with one hand, and the hymnal in his other hand trembled. Beatrice took his arm in support, and Gladys steadied the hymnal. A collective sigh of relief stirred the congregation when a slight breeze moved through the raised stained glass windows. Snow regained his composure.

With the service over, pallbearers elevated the coffin and followed the priest into sunlight. The youth took his mother's elbow. Another parishioner took Hattie's arm. The lady in faded morning stood alone. Beatrice nodded in her direction, and Snow stepped forward to offer his arm. When she looked away, Snow introduced himself, adding, "I was married to Ellen Mae's aunt. I am so sorry for your son's loss."

"I know who you are. I am Carrie Frances Price Darberry." She paused to let her full name reveal family relationships. "We share your loss as well. Jane was always so kind to us. May I express my regret that illness kept me from attending Jane's funeral?" Carrie paused. Snow nodded, vaguely remembering a letter from someone about illness. She resumed, "I was unaware you knew my son's feelings. It is considerate of you to extend your sympathy." They followed the procession without conversation. The lightness of her white-gloved hand on his arm touched the hollow of his loneliness. A twinge radiated across his chest and down his arm.

A short graveside ceremony included a prayer led by James Abbott and a memorial by Thomas. Abbott stepped forward and threw the first shovel of dirt into the grave. Snow only recollected meeting him once, shortly after Abbott eloped with Ellen Mae. The woman and youth with Abbott were unknown to Snow. With whispered gratitude, Richard retrieved his mother from Snow's arm. Snow returned to the Sisters. A lunch prepared by the ladies of the Altar Guild awaited the congregation in a large, renovated boat shed.

First in the receiving line, James Abbott was followed by Thomas, Carrie, and Richard. Mourners addressed her as Aunt Carrie. Abbott waved his companion and the youth toward the family table. The woman sat down peevishly tapping her fan on her palm. Hattie sat at the opposite end of the table.

At the buffet laden with the congregation's best, Snow's appetite peaked. Crispy crab cakes of fresh claw meat lay piled high on platters. New baby peas, finely chopped hard-boiled eggs, crisp bacon bits, and a cold mayonnaise dressing topped a spinach salad. A crowd gathered at the dessert table where Alter Guild members served slices of their secret recipes. While waiting his turn, Snow watched the dwindling receiving line across the room. Carrie Darberry reached for Thomas Coode's arm. Thomas bent his head in Carrie's direction to catch her words. His expression froze. Carrie gripped Thomas sleeve as he pulled away from her. Turning in their direction, Richard was caught unawares. He grasped his mother's arm at the elbow and managed to turn her away from the confrontation. Thomas glared over Carrie's head at Richard. Snow picked up a slice of Gladys Overzee's buttermilk pie, and she smiled triumphantly.

With his filled plate, Snow passed by the family table. Hattie Wells sat contemplating a mourning brooch opened in her hands. On the left side, a lens protected a braid of dark hair. On the right side, a lens protected the miniature portrait.   Anticipating his interest, she lifted the brooch for his inspection.

"My dear Annabelle, she was so full of love and hope. She wanted a better future for me. She wanted to send me away for my education. I refused to leave her." Snow lingered over the image. The tight-lipped smile on a face creased and darkened by fieldwork testified to a hard life. A gentle kindness radiating from the eyes testified to Hattie's memory. Something familiar stared at him out of those eyes.

Hattie sighed. "I miss her so much. When she died, they sent me to live with Ellen Mae. Some nights I hear Annabelle singing in my dreams." Snow's gaze lifted from the brooch to Hattie's eyes, those same eyes.

Thomas joined them and stood behind Hattie with his arms held tightly to his sides. He glared across the room toward Carrie and Richard. Hattie waved her gloved hand at one of the three empty seats and invited Snow to join them. Snow expressed his sympathy and returned the brooch. James Abbott stood filling his plate at the buffet table. Richard, Carrie, and the parishioner who accompanied Hattie to the gravesite still lingered in conversation at the hall door. Snow declined the invitation and explained his promise to sit with the Sisters. Glancing across the room, he saw them watching him. He saw the place of honor saved between them.

The distraction of visitors to the Sister's table prolonged his lunch. Parishioners who had known Jane stopped to express their condolences. Snow's appetite waned. The pie sat uneaten. Uncomfortable with the attention, Snow glanced at the family table. Two places were unoccupied. Richard and Carrie were absent.

The jurist in Snow stirred with

questions. He smiled, remembering Jane's amused, gentle scolding. "William, you put everyone on trial. Someday, I will find myself in that box, and I won't be surprised." Snow decided it was time for a visit to the front room of the Overzee Inn.

Snow Family Tree

William T. Snow II – Anna M. Snow

David Horatio Snow   William T. Snow III
b. 1839   b. 1844
Missing: 1863

Cassin Family Tree

Jacob E. Cassin – Louisa M. Cassin

Jane L. Cassin (Snow)   Ellen Frances Cassin
b. 1846   b. 1842
d. 1902   d. 1862

Coode Family (Cassin and Price Relatives)

Benjamin J. Coode - Eleanor Mae Coode

(Nee Cassin)

b. 1837 d. 1998   b. 1840 d. 1881

Benjamin A. Coode   –   Mary F. Price Coode

b. 1848   d. 1878   b. 1852   d. 1878

Ellen Mae Coode Abbott   Thomas A Coode

b. 1874   d. 1903   b. 1875

Chapter 3: The Front Room

Happy families are all alike; every unhappy family is unhappy in its own way.

Leo Tolstoy, 1828 – 1910

Sultry mist hung over the Patuxent River obscuring the view across to St. Mary's County. Wilted mourners drifted from the funeral lunch seeking shade or a hint of breeze. Snow captured bits of ice left from his lemonade, wrapped them in a handkerchief, and placed it under his summer straw hat. Cool dribbles melted into the cloth and ran down his neck, giving him some relief.

William Snow accompanied the Sisters, who conversed their way across the Island, while he pretended a slight hearing loss. To this, he added walking to the nearest spot of shade and feigning surprise at each delay. Along the way, some Islanders dropped their guard, trading speaking to him for talking about him. Snow turned away. His mind appeared to wander. In fact, he strolled deep in thought, framing questions for his visit to the Overzee's front room.

Eventually, another similarly afflicted gentleman joined Snow in the limited shade of a tulip poplar. The man's wife and four almost grown daughters, trailed by a long-limbed younger son, listened intently to the Sisters' recitations. The two men spent a few moments in companionable silence. Finally, the man offered his hand, opening with, "Your Honor let me extend my sympathies for both the loss of Mrs. Snow and Mrs. Abbott. I am Francis Stump, Constable and Justice of the Peace. May I speak with you for a moment?"

Snow shook Constable Stump's hand. As lingering mourners wandered closer, the constable gave them an annoyed glance.

The two men strolled away, and Stump spoke softly. "I would like to come by the Overzee Inn and visit with you this evening. Might bring someone."

Snow leaned in and nodded, adding, "If you come late when the fireflies light up, I have some excellent Havanas." Stump grunted his consent. Mrs. Stump and her children said their goodbyes. The Sisters watched the constable with interest as he departed several steps behind Mrs. Stump, like a barge in tow.

Back at the Inn, the Sisters were delighted to accommodate Snow's request for refreshments in the front room. In short order, he found himself deep in an overstuffed chair, dripping glass of chilled sassafras tea and Japanese fan in hand. Even the Sisters, set in their ways, had an icebox and received regular deliveries of ice. This kept the Overzee Inn attractive to what the Sisters called "the better trade". By this, they meant tourists who usually stayed at the Seven Gables across the Patuxent River in St. Mary's County.

"Dearest William, please feel free to receive any guests you like in our front room," Beatrice assured him.

Gladys added, "If you tell us when to expect Constable Stump, we could have some refreshments ready." Snow kept his decision to smoke cigars on the screened front porch to himself.

With baited hook, Snow cast his firs questions gently on the waters. "The lady who took my arm after the service, Aunt Carrie, I understand she is actually a cousin and Richard's mother? I thought there was a little more to it."

As her fan fluttered briskly, Beatrice Marie struck the bait first. "Carrie Frances Price Darberry is Ellen Mae's second cousin once removed, seeing as Ellen Mae's mother, Mary Frances Price Coode was first cousin to Carrie's mother, Elisha Danielle Price." She paused and punctuated the air with a swipe of her fan. "That makes Mary Frances Price Coode Carrie's second cousin and her daughter, Ellen Mae, Carrie's second cousin once removed."

Beatrice glanced at Gladys who continued with, "So, you see, Richard Price Darberry and Ellen Mae Coode Abbott are the children of second cousins. That makes Richard, Carrie's son, Ellen Mae's third cousin, and not just the family solicitor."

Snow glanced up from crushing a bit of sugar cube into his sassafras tea. "So, you are telling me Richard Darberry and Ellen Mae Coode Abbott were third cousins." The Sisters nodded in unison.

Beatrice continued. "Old Benjamin Coode lost his son, Young Benjamin, and his daughter-in-law, Mary Frances Price, in the sinking of the steamship Express during the October Gale of '78. After Old Benjamin's wife, Eleanor Mae, your Jane's cousin, died in '81, Carrie came with Little Budd, only five years old. She raised Ellen Mae and her baby brother, Thomas." Snow reflected on the significance of Carrie's absence from the funeral lunch.

On a nod from Beatrice, Gladys picked up the recitation. "You know Carrie never liked people to call Richard "Little Bud". Wanted us all to forget he was the son of Bud Darberry and only remember he was a Price.

Beatrice, folded her fan, and tapped it firmly on the tea table. "And third cousin to Ellen Mae, hoping to make him closer than cousin, too." While fishing through his remaining bits of ice, Snow let the Sisters run with the line of their story.

Gladys nodded. "Quite true, and, one way or another, Carrie took over. She ran the household and family after the grandmother, Eleanor Mae, died."

Beatrice interrupted again. "For years, she led everybody to think Old Benjamin was going to marry her. Of course, that never happened.   Then she tried to convince everyone Ellen Mae and Richard had an understanding. After Ellen Mae eloped with James Abbott, Carrie took to her bed for a week. It serves her right for being so proud with everyone all those years."

"Now, Beatrice," Gladys interrupted. "You know Carrie got that family through some hard times. Had raising those children and running a boat yard all on her shoulders for years with only Little Bud to help. Old Benjamin Coode just fell apart completely over losing his son and then his wife right afterward." Turning to Snow, she continued. "After the Express sinking, Old Benjamin kept answering the door, saying he heard Young Benjamin or saw him coming up the walk. When Carrie came to nurse Old Benjamin's wife, Eleanor Mae, she had just lost her own husband and given up her farm to a lease. If she hadn't dragged Old Benjamin Coode out into the world again, he would have buried himself away in the Elms and never come out until he died. Carrie had nothing, and she held them all together all those years. She had a right to expect more than she got."

Gladys leaned forward, fanning with greater flurry, and seemed about to interrupt again. Sitting taller and lifting slightly from her seat, Beatrice seemed about to pull her disappearing act. But, Gladys sat back looking into the distance, and Beatrice leaned back in her chair. A silent truce settled over them.

Lost in the vision of Old Benjamin forcibly dragged from the Elms into the world, Snow recalled the scent of Jane's roses. He smiled over the chilled glass rim and redirected the conversation with "You have a lovely garden. Such fragrant roses."

Eyebrows raised, the Sisters glanced at each other. A mutual decision not to mention the lack of roses at the Overzee passed silently between them. Beatrice offered Snow more ice chipped from the small block in a towel wrapped bucket. He asked, "How did Carrie loose her husband?"

Gladys advanced into the new story line. "Well, Richard Enoch Darberry, called Bud, married Carrie after she inherited her father's farm. Bud was five years younger than Carrie, from a big family of watermen, and didn't have any prospects. So, he took what he could get and that was Carrie, homely and sour as she was. Then they couldn't make the Price farm, over on St. Mary's River, pay. So, they moved back with Bud's family when his pa died. Bud sublet one mail route from Valley Lee to Piney Point and another to St. George's Island."

Beatrice jumped in with, "It was a good income and they were saving for more land. Bud had a pair of mules and a wagon, and it was 16 miles twice a week. He made $187 a year for those routes. Strange enough, the same storm that sunk the Express killed him, too. Bud ran his routes at night because the mail didn't get to Valley Lee until after 10 o'clock. He worked on the water and the farm during the day. Carrie said the mules knew the way in the dark and Bud could just about sleep the whole trip. Something happened in all the wind and rain that night. The wagon tipped over."

Gladys picked up her lines with, "Beatrice isn't telling you Bud used to go and drink at Trappe's Tavern early before the mail arrived. He slept while the mules took the wagon back, mostly by themselves and well before breakfast. Only a drunk would try to deliver the mail in that storm."

Beatrice rose to Bud's defense. "No one knew how bad that storm would be. There were wind gusts over 100 miles per hour. Even the Potomac Transportation

Company said they didn't know, or they wouldn't have sent the Express out in it. Anyway, Carrie lost the mail routes and had to rent her land to a relative of Bud's. Mr. Coode needed her to come, and she needed somewhere to go. In the end, Old Benjamin Coode sent Richard to St. John's and later to the University Of Maryland School Of Law. Richard would never have gotten his education but for Old Benjamin. Then Richard came back and started a practice here."

"There's no practice here." Gladys sniffed. "Richard has an office at the Coode Yard and mostly helps run things for the family. Sometimes he draws up wills, and titles, and the like for others, but he takes vegetables, chickens and such in trade if you can't pay. Once in a while, he represents somebody in the circuit court, but he usually wants money up front for that. Carrie had ideas Richard might marry Ellen Mae someday. That's why she convinced Old Benjamin to send Ellen Mae to St. Mary's Academy over in Leonardtown instead of St. Catherine's up in Baltimore. Carrie thought she could control things from down here, but you can see that didn't work out. Ellen Mae eloped with the friend of a lay teacher. Carrie's been most unhappy about it for all these years. Then Old Benjamin died. Ellen Mae would have turned Carrie out, but Old Benjamin put it in his will Carrie could live there as long as Ellen Mae kept the Elms. All Carrie has to go back to is the old farm she rents out. Snow recalled Carrie's faded mourning dress and considered the possible cause of Ellen Mae's ingratitude toward the woman who raised her.

A pause in conversation hovered like the haze across the Patuxent River. The Sisters peered across the road at shapes in the shifting mist along the shore.

Snow waited, but they were going to make him ask. He asked, "Where does

Richard live?"

Gladys leaned forward in whispered conspiracy. "For years, he lived right there at the Elms with Carrie. Then, when Ellen Mae married, he moved into a room next to his office behind the Coode Yard sail loft."

Beatrice snapped. "Now he lives in a cottage behind the yard, where James Abbott's sister lived before she moved across Back Creek. He's too good a son to leave Carrie, and she won't leave the Elms."

A memory of Carrie brushing lint from Richard's sleeve came back to Snow. This simple act of parental love, a love he and Jane never experienced, stirred a spasm of grief. A deep, double sigh rose from his lungs. He had forgotten to breathe.

In the distance, along the misty shore, Snow could see a couple walking. The woman clung to her partner's arm. The man leaned towards her in intimate conversation.   A memory of something silken brushed Snow's face. A memory of lavender scent in Jane's hair came to him.

"I'm sure Jane told me of Ellen Mae's courtship and marriage, but I am not always such a good listener." He smiled wrapping his handkerchief around the cool, dripping glass.

Gladys leaned forward, whispering. "Yes.   Well, we see now that you are getting the point."

Beatrice struck with, "James Abbott is from West Virginia, so we don't actually know him." She paused long enough for Snow to appreciate the Sisters' appraisal of Abbott as a stranger still.

Gladys continued Abbott's known history with, "James Abbott claimed distant relations in Baltimore who were Lathmores. He claimed them as second cousins, but he had a letter of introduction from his mother when he arrived. None of the Baltimore Lathmores had ever met him.

Seems his mother had left for West Virginia with a soldier from Point Lookout Prison after the Great Rebellion. Of course, her parents didn't approve, and then she married another man. So, the Lathmores have no idea what happened to her. Died about the time James introduced himself to his Baltimore cousins, perhaps before, but probably after."

Beatrice continued the tale. "James Abbott came to Leonardtown, over in St. Mary's County, where he knew a lay teacher at St. Mary's Academy. Quite improperly, without Old Benjamin's permission, the teacher introduced James Abbott to Ellen Mae. At seventeen, She eloped with him thinking he would take her away and show her the world. As a destitute man of 27 years, he saw an opportunity to settle down well." Beatrice hesitated, sipping her sassafras tea and waving her fan at an intruding insect.

Snow forced a small cough to loosen a tightness growing in his chest.

Gladys took up the account with, "In the end, when the threats were over, Ellen Mae didn't get to see the world. James Abbott surprised everyone by taking over management of the shipyard. Then, he turned a good profit, expanded the business, and gained Old Benjamin's affections. There never were any children from that marriage. All this was before little Hattie was brought to live at the Elms." The Sisters lapsed into silence, sipping their tea, waiting. With his forehead cooling under the wet handkerchief, Snow nibbled ice captured along the rim of his glass. He let the silence flow on like a lazy summer stream.

Gladys fanned slowly and sighed with impatience. Beatrice folded her fan and finished the tale. "About two years later, James brought his sister, Annie Clarke, with her invalid, idiot husband and difficult son, to live behind the Coode Boatyard. A loud argument about the boy resulted in James moving Annie Clarke and her family across Back Creek. James still provides for their support."

White oaks whispered with the breeze dissipating the mist. The strolling couple, no longer arm in arm, came clearly into focus. They faced each other in earnest conversation. The distance between them grew wider. Abruptly, Hattie folded her arms, turned, and walked back towards Avondale. The three occupants of the Overzee's porch watched Thomas closely as he made his way towards them. Beatrice prepared him a glass of sassafras tea. Gladys prepared to pounce. Neither of the Sisters paid attention as Snow excused himself.

In shade at the back of the Inn, Snow wandered out along its empty pier. From the farthest piling, a lone osprey ruffled its feathers. It glared at him possessively, before lifting off and skimming the creek to Molly's Leg. The tiny overgrown island, with a long abandoned pauper's graveyard and scrub oaks, created an ideal nesting area. Snow leaned against a piling. It gave some under his weight, almost ready to topple into Back Creek. He chose another judiciously rocking it first.

Glints of sunlight flashing off the creek drowned out reflected light from objects along the shore. A woman strode purposefully toward the Overzee's back entrance. At a distance, Hattie formed a shifting, shimmering silhouette of shadow backlit by a dancing dazzle of light. Moving closer, she observed Snow standing on the pier and halted. Her stiffened posture reminded Snow of the osprey. Turning away from him, she strolled back along the water's edge and stopped in a bit of shade. She waited, her backlit form darkly obscured. A tall figure in top hat joined her. She continued to stare in

Snow's direction as if he were in her way. Eventually, she took Richard's arm and let him escort her towards Avondale. Snow noted how easily she moved from the arm of one man to another. Rubbing the tingling in his arm, he decided on a nap.

Upstairs, a breeze pushed through from the oaks and did its best to cool the room. The soft ticking of the clock distracted his thoughts. He checked the hour and noticed how the elegant, rosewood, six-column, mantel clock seemed foreign among worn furnishing of the old inn. Resting, Snow took long deep breaths to relieve the consistent pressure growing in his chest.

Snows Rest, A Maryland Mystery

L. A. Stewart

Chapter 4: The Visitor

Time isn't measured by length but by depth.
Isolde Kurz, 1853 – 1944

Snow woke when the rosewood mantle clock struck 6:00. After sponging off the day's heat with tepid water from the washstand pitcher, he put a clean, round-tipped collar on his shirt. Then he walked past empty rooms and went down to a light supper.

Alone, Gladys emerged from the kitchen to serve his solitary meal in uncharacteristic silence. Pungent aroma of buttered spinach, crowned by limp bacon bits and chopped hard cooked egg, hung in the humid dining room with an air of second life. Snow picked with disappointment. Only a creamy, cornmeal spoon bread drizzled with honey saved the meal. He consumed it with a concentration that even tepid coffee couldn't break. Retreating to the screened front porch and one of Captain Gourley's Cuban cigars, he waited.

A crescendo of chorusing cicadas faded revealing the distant notes of an exotic, ragged music floating from another inn along the waterfront. Fireflies bobbed and blinked across the misted yard. The tip of Snow's cigar glowed as the evening darkened. In deepening shadows, boys appeared and ran together between houses, sometimes dragging a stick along the clapboard sides. Two men walked across the bridge from Avondale. They strolled along the oyster shell road, leaning towards each other in quiet conspiracy. The shadow boys abruptly retreated behind houses, regrouping after the pair passed. Snow felt in his shirt pocket for two of Gourley's cigars. The men came up the porch steps, and Constable Stump introduced Dr. Radcliff. Snow recognized the doctor as the parishioner who escorted Hattie to Ellen Mae's grave.

After introductions, Snow offered cigars. Silence accompanied the lengthy ritual of snipping, striking, lighting, and drawing air. Distant ragtime, piano notes rose in staccato tempo to a climax and fell away to silence. Fragrant smoke drifted into the night until the cigars were a half inch gone before Constable Stump opened the business of the visit.

"There's been talk, long time, 'bout a railroad coming all the way down the county." Stump paused, working on his cigar. Snow nodded. After every severe winter, the Pennsylvania Railroad looked for a port that might not freeze over as quickly as Baltimore. Landowners hoped they'd get good money for their land if the rails went through it.

Stump exhaled a ring. "Surprised to hear land agents were on Coode land around Chesapeake Beach. A waterman came to me about it yesterday evening. Seems he mentioned the land agents to James Abbott when he brought his skipjack to the Coode Yard for repairs. Abbott was surprised. Got all red and angry. Next thing, the waterman hears Mrs. Abbott is dead." The understated tone of Stump's words did nothing to soften Snow's astonishment. With his cigar hovering halfway to his mouth, Snow stared at Stump in disbelief.

Dr. Radcliff shifted in his chair. Stump looked sideways at him and waited. Radcliff began with, "It might be possible that the sale had already taken place. When I arrived at the funeral luncheon, I overheard Richard talking to his mother. Mrs. Darberry asked about money from the sale of land. Carrie Darberry is a patient of mine, so I offered my sympathy and asked after her health. Carrie told me that Ellen Mae had money from the sale of land to the railroad, but no one could find it. Richard was visibly upset with her and said he would talk to me later. They left the luncheon without eating." Snow drew on his cigar and tapped the ash into a spittoon the Sisters kept on the porch.

Constable Stump leaned forward and directed his attention to Snow. "Could Ellen Mae sell land without Abbott knowing 'bout it?"

Snow exhaled slowly, delaying his reply. "If a married woman inherited land, she would need her husband's permission to sell it, as it would belong to him also. Does that answer your question?" Dissatisfied, both visitors fell into silence.

Snow took advantage of the silence with, "Let me ask you a question, Constable. Wouldn't Thomas have to know about any land sale? As Old Benjamin's heir, he would have inherited also."

Radcliff concentrated on his cigar, rolling it between his fingers. Stump half closed his eyes and looked sidewise at

Radcliff before responding with, "Thomas fell out with Old Benjamin. Got himself cut out of the will." The three men drew on their cigars. Snow thought the taciturn constable had finished, but Stump continued. "When Thomas was 'bout 20, he killed a man in a bar fight over a girl. Thomas went into the army. Happened before I became constable." Snow gazed into the haze-filtered moonlight, sifting Stump's revelation into the Sisters' account of Thomas' fall from grace.

Radcliff shifted in his chair and changed the subject with, "On Friday afternoon, Hattie Wells came to my office. She told me Ellen Mae slipped on a spill in the kitchen and hit her head. Hattie said Ellen Mae was putting up strawberry preserves. I've seen numerous head injuries from boat accidents, and they usually bleed badly. Sometimes there is a fractured skull, and they bleed subcutaneously. When I arrived, Ellen Mae lay on the couch in the front room, where James had moved her. A small amount of blood congealed in her hair at the back of her head. Her scalp had two patches of torn hair, one on each side. James claims that she hit her head against the iron stove after slipping on a broken jar of strawberry preserves. Strawberry preserves smeared her dress front. I had been treating Ellen Mae for other symptoms. None of these were likely to be fatal, so I assumed the fall had killed her."

A slight breeze drifted through the screened porch. Cigar embers glowed, and smoke blew away in lazy curls across the porch disbursing around the corner. Snow weighed his words, unsure if he wanted to get any further into this speculation. "What other symptoms?"

The doctor drew himself up. "The patient complained of nausea that increased over time. As a result, she lost weight. She had a blue tone to her skin and difficulty breathing. Another time, she developed Bradycardia, a slow heartbeat. Oddly, the whites of her eyes had a slightly jaundiced cast. Xanthopsia is not a symptom of comfrey use, but the use of a different herbal remedy. In an elderly patient, the symptoms aren't unusual. They are unusual in a young woman. Arthritis is also unusual for someone her age, but it runs in the family. Someone gave her comfrey tea for arthritis. After I advised her to use comfrey as a compress but not to drink it, the blue tone of her skin went away. The other symptoms continued occasionally. In the last week, before her death, the blue skin tone returned. Ellen Mae hadn't summoned me to the house in three months. So, I don't know if she was drinking the tea or how advanced her symptoms had become."

The jurist in Snow stirred. "If you hadn't been to the house in three months, how did you know Ellen Mae's skin tone was blue again?"

"Hattie told me when she assisted me on my general clinic days. Hattie wants to take up nursing. She can recite the Nightingale Pledge, and has ideas about going to New York to study home nursing with Lillian Wald." Radcliff smiled indulgently.

Stump interrupted with, "When Hattie came for you, did you go into the Elms through the kitchen?"

Radcliff rolled his cigar between his fingers and nodded. "Yes. The back entry is closer to my house, so I went into the kitchen and walked through to the front parlor. Ellen Mae lay on the sofa, unconscious with a slowing erratic pulse. She never recovered. About 5 minutes after my arrival, her breathing stopped, and she passed. Blue tinged the edges of the mouth again. Her scalp at the lower back of her head had a wound with some blood in her hair. Blood smeared the stove corner, but I didn't notice it until I went back through on my way out."

"Was glass broken underfoot or blood on the floor?" Snow asked sharply. After a moment, Ratcliff shook his head no and slumped in his chair.

"Could the blue around her mouth and erratic pulse result from drinking comfrey tea?" Snow adopted a judicial tone. Ratcliff sat straighter.

"No, knitbone, that is comfrey, causes liver failure. Some of Ellen Mae's symptoms were like those of foxglove use." Ratcliff added, "When first calling on her, I asked if she was using foxglove. She said no. I warned her sternly against it."

Stump sat slumped over his cigar and watched something in the distant, misty evening. "Cannin' in the kitchen seems odd. Mrs. Stump does cannin' out back in summer. Has an old stove out in the yard. Must have been impossible hot in that kitchen. What did you list as the cause of death?"

"I intended to list it as accidental death due to a fall. Now that I've had time to think about it..."

Snow sat up, cigar ash falling onto porch floorboards. "You haven't issued a death certificate yet, but we have had a funeral and a will read?"

Radcliff spun his cigar, shaking his head. "No... I mean that's right. I don't know if there was a will, or if it was read."

"Did Richard Darberry talk to you after the service, as he said he would?" Snow was incredulous at the direction Radcliff's suspicions were taking them.

"Richard said he'd be by this afternoon. I waited, thinking he would come by for the death certificate, as he is the family solicitor. We would talk then. When he didn't, I went to the Elms. No one was there. I went to the Coode Yard office, but I saw James Abbott rowing his sister home across Back Creek. She lives on the point with her son and husband."

"Did you check Richard's cottage?" Snow's concern grew. Radcliff shook his head no and shrugged at the same time.

"I don't remember seeing a husband at the funeral." Snow raised an eyebrow at Radcliff.

Radcliff plodded on. "The husband, Arthur Clark, suffered a head injury in a boating accident years ago. James brought them all down here. At first, they lived in a cottage behind the boatyard. Later James moved them across the creek. Arthur never comes over this side. I treated him a few times when I rowed over on house calls." Snow waited for Radcliff to continue, but the doctor lapsed into silence.

Eventually, Snow asked, "Doctor, when you said blue skin and shortness of breath were not unusual in an elderly patient, were you referring to a particular patient?"

"Mr. Coode, Old Benjamin Coode. He had those symptoms, but he had a failing heart."

"And could it be possible that a fall was the cause of Ellen Mae's death?"

Radcliff nodded, shrugging again. "But I'm thinking it less likely than when I first saw her. Her skin was blue again, and the head injury didn't appear traumatic enough to have caused an immediate death. If there had been slow internal bleeding of the brain, death might have occurred after a period, let's say a few days of unconsciousness."

Stump looked obliquely at Snow. "I was hoping, as a member of the family, you could shed some light on Ellen Mae's health. You could have knowledge of the will and land transactions?"

Snow searched his memory. "My connection to the Coode family was distant. Mrs. Snow visited them in the summer on her way to Snows Rest, but I was not able to join her on those occasions. I came down later when the court was not in session. Sometimes, Ellen Mae would visit us in Baltimore and bring Hattie with her. They spent most of the time in Mrs. Snow's company." Stump was leaning forward now, looking directly into Snow's eyes, searching. After an uncomfortable pause, Stump looked out across the river, a big man keeping his own counsel.

Cigar smoke rose and spiraled into the still air of a sultry night. A long-limbed boy came down the road, silhouetted in moonlight and separated from the other boys who hid in shadows. Skillfully, the boy rattled a rusted, old wagon wheel rim along the road, balancing it on a stick, back and forth, back and forth. In front of the Overzee Inn, he let the rim fall and looked toward the porch.

"Mrs. Stump is wondering when I'll be home." Stump rose and ended the interview.

Snow spoke last. "I will sail for St. Mary's tomorrow. If I remember anything of interest, I will let you know." The youth vanished into darkness. The visitors departed, and Snow sat in contemplation, as he finished his cigar. Why had he come here to this funeral? After all these years of avoiding this side of Jane's family, why had he come now? Stubbing out the cigar, he stood, stretched his legs, and surveyed the Overzee's barren yard in moonlight. He commented aloud that flowerbeds and a few rose bushes might attract more clients. Then, he realized he was alone.

Going in, Snow felt a shadow drift from the front room through the dining room and out through the kitchen. He followed it and found the Sisters were fanning themselves in unison on the back stoop. Sitting on a lower step, Snow leaned against the iron pipe railing and looked out across Back Creek. Strains of a distant piano playing "The Maple Leaf Rag" drifted from somewhere among the inns and bars.

Condensation ran down a pitcher of liquid the Sisters shared in tin cups. Beatrice offered to get Snow a cup, but he declined. Time passed in silence, and he shifted his weight as if to leave.

Gladys Hope began in the middle of her thought. "The steamship Express went down on October 23rd in 1878. Eighteen of 31 crew and passengers were lost. He has no memory of his parents. The only one who ever loved him was his grandmother, Eleanor Mae, your Jane's cousin. Thomas lost her when he was six. That was when Carrie came to care for them, bringing Richard with her. She was always quick to point out Thomas' faults to Old Benjamin while promoting Richard, of course."

"Not that it mattered much." Beatrice picked up the story. "Old Benjamin favored Ellen Mae over all of them because she reminded him of his wife, Eleanor.

Thomas, with his red hair, reminded Benjamin of his drowned daughter-in-law, Mary Frances Price Coode. Old Benjamin always thought his son had married beneath him, but his opinion was no match against a young man's fancy for a beautiful girl."

"Old Benjamin never knew what a jewel Young Benjamin had found." Gladys nodded toward Snow in the dark.

Beatrice went on. "Thomas rebelled against his grandfather by quitting school and working in the boat yard when he was about ten. Or maybe Old Benjamin sent him to work, thinking he had no better future. That was one time when Carrie came to his defense. She wouldn't let him work on the boats in the yard. She insisted he work in the office as an assistant clerk, helping keep the books."

The Sisters paused, each refilling the other's cup. Gladys continued, "At 13, Thomas went to work on the *John E.*

Tygert, a steamer out of Baltimore, assistant to the clerk no less. In about seven years, Thomas worked his way up to purser of the *Potomac*. I remember, because he was just 21 when he got into that trouble."

A breeze picked up, finally giving some respite from the heat. Questions turned around in Snow's mind. He tried to word them so as not to reveal his ignorance.

Beatrice sat up taller to give herself height. "I really think he was 22 or 23 by then, Gladys, and that was how he got into the cavalry. After the trouble, he ran away and enlisted to avoid charges. James Abbott gave Thomas money to buy horses so he could join the cavalry instead of ending up a foot soldier. Remember, he could shoot real well, and even rose up to be a sergeant in one year?"

"No, Beatrice, he didn't make sergeant until he got in those Rough Riders. He knew someone from Charles County who got him in because they all hunted with Theodore Roosevelt. He made sergeant after they charged up Kettle Hill in that big battle."

"No, Gladys. He never was in that battle, 'cause his horse fell on him the day before and tore up his knee. He still limps from that."

A truce fell between them, as they thought it over. "Well, maybe you're right, but he's still a hero with medals, even if he didn't ride up that hill." Gladys made peace.

Cooler air flowed through the yard, carrying the smell of a storm. Snow went up to his room wondering about Thomas Alexius Coode. Being a hero seemed to have expunged his guilt.

Sometime in the night, crashing thunder and lightning rolled over the island, shaking the Overzee Inn. Rising to shut out the torrent, Snow noticed soft light from windows below falling into the rain soaked yard. He shuffled across the hall and down the stairs, expecting to find the Sisters drawn together against the din. He didn't hear the suppressed tones of Chopin until the mid-level landing. Graced by low lantern light, two figures were just visible at the upright piano. A gleaming, ebony back and large muscled arms played the melody gently. One delicate arm reached out from under long black tresses, contentedly resting across the broad shoulders. Above the loosely drawn, cotton camisole, the other ivory arm reached out to play a chord. The two bodies graced each other with familiarity. Quietly, they worked their duet beneath the roar and thunder of nature. An indigo blue cotton jacket lay folded on the piano bench. Frozen on the landing, Snow waited for the next thunder crash to cover his retreat. At the other end of the hall, a guest room door clicked shut.

L. A. Stewart

Chapter 5: Going Home

It is always darkest just before the day dawneth.
Thomas Fuller, 1608 – 1661

Birdcalls heralded dawn and summer's approaching heat. Not bothering to shave, Snow shoved soiled clothing into his trunk and left in the front hall. Then he walked down the back hall for a kitchen breakfast of cold ham and biscuits. The coffee had a trace of mint but was otherwise weak. Through the kitchen screen door, Snow watched his skipjack, *Louisa Mae*. Newly arrived, she rose and fell in gentle swells at the Overzee's pier. Two silhouettes in gray light sat on the skipjack's cabin. John Lundy, caretaker at Snows Rest, and Paul, John's son, became more distinct in the rising light. Born a slave, John was manumitted at age 10 by Snow's father. Snow, his older brother David, and John were close as boys. There would be talk of business with John on the sail down to the Rest. Snow ate at leisure. He glanced out the back screen door several times. Gladys, following those glances, cleared Snow's plate and offered only more coffee.

"Breakfast, well, we gave them breakfast. But, they wouldn't come in."

"Are you just speaking about this morning?" Snow remarked into his coffee.

Gladys flushed and bustled into the dining room. Dishes rattled as the sisters set a table for boarders who might come on the next steamboat. Snow knew there would be few if any. Affluence flooded and ebbed through the creeks and rivers of the southern counties. The laced and pristine, empty rooms of the Overzee sat marooned in the past. For most of the island, business improved but not at the Overzee. The price of coffee was up to .35/lb. The Sisters would not present a bill to family, but Snow left four extra greenbacks with his usual payment under the sugar bowl. The screen door creaked, and a muffled thank you followed him. With a hand raised in farewell, he ambled out to the *Louisa Mae*. His trunk rested in the skipjack's cabin.

John guided the 36-foot skipjack into Back Creek through puffs of wind and took them out past Molly's Leg. With coaxing, the *Louisa Mae* slipped out of the creek and into the Patuxent River. Halfway across, John tacked her over to a starboard tack and headed into the Chesapeake. John's stoic silence as he set the course contrasted with Paul's constant tapping and humming as he trimmed the sails. Well out into the Bay, they tacked over and fell off to a reach along the shore. A sense of belonging flooded into Snow's soul, a sense of going home. He lay down on his back along the starboard gunnel, his summer straw over his face. An ease swept over him as winds lightened, and the *Louisa Mae* drifted south.

Sunlight beat down on their heads and reflected off the water. They were making little progress when Snow returned to the cockpit. A hint of cool air, gliding over the port beam, gave little relief. The *Louisa Mae* picked up a half knot in slack sails. Snow ordered John to tack back over to starboard and head across the Bay towards the Eastern Shore, hoping for wind in that direction. With a glance astern, John ignored Snow and hugged the St. Mary's shoreline. The helm wandered, stalling the boat's progress. Several craft with deep drafts and double masts made across the Bay toward Oxford. One boat, a bugeye ten feet longer than Snow's skipjack, followed the *Louisa Mae*'s course. The two craft drifted south through light wind toward Point No Point. Paul checked the bugeye's progress, as its longer waterline and greater sail area steadily closed the distance. A pine twig lay in the gunnel, and he jettisoned it to check the *Louisa Mae*'s speed. The twig bobbed along within reach for several minutes before drifting away in current. He glanced impatiently at his father.

John and the bugeye's helmsman held their course. Perhaps, they both smelled wind shifts and felt the electric prickle of storms before God or the Devil thought them up. Several minutes of complete calm preceded a coiling current of air. The ripple of cat's paws, gliding across the water, encircled the prey.

Snow sat up. Small hairs rose on the back of his neck. Still, he was unprepared for the cannon shot and concussion of the first assailing strike. Over the ridgeline of trees, a blow of heavy weather unfurled above them. Froth topped waves grasped the hull where only moments before glassy reflections had returned their gaze. As the hull lifted and rolled, John's steady hand brought the *Louisa Mae* into the wind. He surfed a wave shoreward, rolling it out from under them. Other waves assailed the *Louisa Mae's* hull like lines of combatants determined to roll her over. They set a course for St. Jerome's Creek, the nearest shelter. Paul dropped the foresail and reefed down the main. Snow raised the centerboard enough to avoid grounding the skipjack on oyster shoals. Still, the *Louisa Mae* gained headway, racing into the creek. Green flashes, exploding from blackened sky, revealed the channel to safety as the deluge fell in sheets obscuring the fate of the Bay. They sliced into the creek and the hull skipped sand on the shallow creek bed. Snow's sense of ease vanished into awe for the hand of God.

"Tide's low," was John's only remark. Father and son grinned at each other in the moment's relief.

When the bugeye followed them into

the channel, John headed into shallows where the bugeye couldn't follow. He gave Paul a hard look. "Cards are the devil's work."

The squall passed down the Bay almost as quickly as the flash of anger passed across Paul's face. The horizon cleared, and he countered with, "I do not use cards to make my way in the world." In that exchange was the quarrel between country labor and urban leisure, the variance of generations. Meticulously removing his money belt from under his shirt, Paul leaned over and placed it in a carpetbag below along with his shoes.

"Where you goin?" John muttered. Paul's jaws clenched as he stepped over the gunnels. He disembarked the *Louisa Mae* into shallows without rocking the skipjack and wadded towards the tree lined creek bank. John slipped the locker hasp open, lifted the lid, and unwrapped a rifle, without taking his eyes off the bugeye.

"Too far. You'll miss.", Snow stated flatly. John left the locker lid open.

The crew of the bugeye took interest only in Paul. They watched him proceed open-handed and unhurried along the shoreline, his large muscled shoulders and long arms relaxed. One of the crew pointed, called out something. The others became animated and friendly. "Piano Paul" drifted across the creek.

John made a humpf sound, gazing into the corn and tobacco fields lining the opposite bank. "Corn's short. Tabacca's thin. Needs more rain. Won't be 'nough corn come winter." Snow took him to mean at the Rest, knowing John had made an opening salvo on the subject of business.

With the *Louisa Mae* held hostage, Paul nattered at length with the bugeye's crew. When he came away, leisurely retracing his steps, he held a quilt wrapped bundle under his arm. Wading back through the shallows, he stepped smoothly aboard. A nod passed between father and son. Without comment, Paul gently unfolded the tattered quilt and ran his hand thoughtfully over the contents.

"Judge Snow, the Misses Oversee sent this clock you left." Snow frowned at the elegant rosewood mantel clock. Perplexed, he took it from Paul and rewrapped it. A foot tall and a half foot longer, its mechanism issued muffled ticking sounds. Snow placed it in his trunk, carefully packing his clothing around the quilt. The bugeye sailed out of the creek. John got the *Louisa Mae* underway.

Silence rained down all the way past the cottages of Scotland Beach to Point Lookout. They made good headway, tacking across the path of several smaller craft. John drove south with a good wind on the beam. Lost in his own thoughts, Paul trimmed sail, occasionally glancing at Snow's trunk. Snow, on the last leg of a trip to the past, was determined to keep memories from overwhelming his purpose.

They tacked over into shifting light winds as the *Louisa Mae* sailed around Point Lookout. Here the wide mouth of the Potomac separated Maryland from Virginia as swirling currents rushed into the Chesapeake Bay. Site of a civil war prison camp and hospital, as well as numerous storms and disasters, the point and lighthouse were subjects of legendary hauntings. Here the ghosts of Confederate soldiers were said to wander beaches at night. Here the ghost of James Heaney, second mate on the steamer Express, sunk in the Gale of '78, wandered the shoreline searching for survivors. Here Old Benjamin Coode lost his son, Young Benjamin, and daughter-in-law, Mary Frances. The *Louisa Mae* rounded the point and sailed north past the peace of Cornfield Harbor. In dying air up St. Mary's River, they drifted slowly past St. Mary's Seminary for Woman. One lone sail appeared far astern on the same course.

After rounding a sandy point sheltering Snows Run, John raised the centerboard. An old meandering dock, with a small flat-bottomed dory tied to one piling, came into view. The *Louisa Mae* drifted a long tedious way toward the dock. Snow recollected his youthful arrogance when approaching this dock with plenty of headway on, pumping the rudder and backing the foresail to stall. Back then, the centerboard needed pulling only a few yards away on a low tide. Rain, snowmelt, floods, tides running and ebbing: all silted the cove up until the way of all things slowed. Change was everywhere, especially when you least wanted it. A sliver of pain drifted across his shoulder and down one arm.

A crumbling, receding shoreline required new planking to connect the old dock to land. As they walked from old dock to new dock to the shore, Snow glanced up out of habit. A deeply embedded chain dangled from the trunk of a venerable oak. Yards overhead a few rusted links hung from that tree where an ancient anchor chain, now grown into the tree, hid under the bark. Leaning out over the cove, the tree curved up toward the light. Not all the upper limbs had leafed out. Centuries before Snow's time, English ships with expensive goods to trade for timber and tobacco tied up with the chain. Now the chain had grown high with the tree and deep into its wood. Snow always looked for it. Someday, the tree would fall into the creek. Would he still be here to search for the chain? On impulse, he started to salute the oak but ended swatting at a fly.

On the road up hill, clay slid underfoot, slick from recent rain but hard below the surface from a long drought. An ominous sucking sound came with each step like the earth giving warning. See the rows of brown-tipped tobacco plantings and stunted corn stalks, it said. Look at three old barns, two leaning. Isn't the stripping house bulging at one side? Snow scrutinized the barns, assessed the need, and slowed his pace. He stopped to examine a stunted tobacco leaf and moved on.

"Rows need tending", he said over his shoulder. John dropped back a few paces, adjusted Snow's trunk from one shoulder to another, and resisted Paul's attempt to hoist it to broader shoulders. Snow walked down a row of withering corn sprouts, made a point of pulling weeds, walked back out, and continued up the road.

On the hill ahead, Snow's Rest endured a sagging roof. Snow kept his eyes down to avoid twisting an ankle in the rutted road. His straw hat shaded his face from the sun already steaming morning's insufficient rainfall from parched plants. Eventually, the travelers arrived at the front entrance. John deftly set the chest just inside the front door and went around the back where a summer kitchen sat separate from the house. Paul followed. Snow turned to view sunlight on the river in time to see a smaller boat sail up the St. Mary's with three passengers.

With his mud-caked shoes left in the foyer, Snow shuffled into the front room and the silence of his memories. A small, cabinet-card photograph sat between two prized porcelain dogs on the fireplace mantel. Dressed in a navy linen suit and white wedding veil, Jane had refused to look somberly into the camera. Instead, she gazed lovingly up at Snow as they leaned on a Brady stand to hold their pose. Snow set the photograph on a table in front of the sofa and sat to rest awhile.

Snow dozed, heard the clicking of hounds' untrimmed claws on the foyer's brick floor. He woke with a start to discover only the ticking of the mantel clock winding down inside the trunk. Pulling it out and unfolding the quilt, he opened the back intending to lock the mechanism. The bottom panel shifted under his touch. Contents of a false bottom spilled over the floor. His surprise echoed through the solitude. A sudden chill of premonition crept up his spine, inched across his shoulder, and down his arm. Holding his breath, Snow listened to the old house creaking. Finally, he unfolded letters and a bill of sale for land to the Baltimore and Ohio Railroad from around an embroidered linen purse. The purse opened and money in large bills spilled over the floor. His breath and thoughts came erratically. Possibilities flooded through his mind, as he positioned the clock on the fireplace mantel. With the clock's contents collected, he mounted the stairs on silent stocking feet to the master bedroom.

There he disappeared. A false wall of removable boards concealed a ladder down to a tunnel below the front room fireplace. It led out to the ruins of a storehouse. Here in this tunnel, his ancestors had hid and kept valuables safe from pirates and British soldiers. Once used as a colonial port of entry, the storehouse had long ago crumbled into its foundation, sealing the tunnel at one end. Snow quietly retraced his steps back through the tunnel and returned to the front room. There he helped himself to three fingers of his favorite Melrose Rye, a Maryland blend of five whiskeys created by Harry Goldsborough in 1885.

Later, John's wife, Sarah, brought Snow a light meal of cold crab and chicken with biscuits. He ate on the front porch and watched the river. The cooler breeze of evening swept away the insects. Fortified with supper and three more fingers of rye, he visited the Snow family cemetery behind the unkempt formal gardens. He read inscriptions starting with the oldest still legible on worn sandstone. Some had hearts for God's love, and some had stars for all things under heaven. His parent's gravestone was white marble with a carving of an urn under a willow. William Thomas Snow II, who freed the slaves of Snow's Rest before the Emancipation Proclamation, rested in peace. Next to him lay Edna Maud Snow, who encouraged their eldest son, David, to join the Army of Northern Virginia. Swept with unease, he read his brother's memorial.

David Horatio Snow
September 3, 1839 - May 6, 1863
The noble youth with soul of fire,
Alive to duty's thrilling cry.

Abruptly, he moved on to Jane who rested separate from the others among her roses. Wafting in the scent of those roses and lit by the intermittent sparkle of fireflies, it seemed the most romantic place in the world. A memory of Jane's voice, reading aloud in the summer evening, whispered to him. She read from an Austen novel, "to lighten his soul with romance". He sighed, missing the perfection of life with Jane Cawsin Snow on his arm.

Darkness with its symphony of cicadas sent Snow in to bed with his bottle of rye for company. By then, the trunk was in his bedroom. Screened windows, on opposite sides of the room, let the scent of roses through. Snow latched the door, balanced two iron doorstops atop each other in its path, and listened. As the sounds of night enfolded Snows Rest, he again descended the dank, hidden stairs. By the light of a candle, he counted $8,723 in the embroidered purse.   All the bills dated from before 1870. This fortune was the value of land sold to the Baltimore and Ohio Railroad by Benjamin Thomas Coode. This was the value of land needed for bridge construction along the Metropolitan Line between Washington and Point of Rocks. More than a boat yard owner, Old Benjamin was a successful land speculator. Among the letters, one dated this April from the Pennsylvania Railroad.   It expressed interest in exploring Ellen Mae's offer of land between Chesapeake Beach and Solomon's Island. Every creak of Snow's ascent from hiding screeched through the house. In his bedroom, Snow reached into the trunk and removed a leather case containing his Colt Sport Model 1902.   Hefted in his hand, it weighed less than the Remington 1860 he used against Jeb Stuart's Third Brigade at Chancellorsville on May 6th of '63.

L. A. Stewart

Chapter 6: Snows Rest

Only the dead have seen an end to war.
Bertrand Russell, 1872 - 1970

Snow drifts in dreams and shallow sleep. A snare drum beats, right, left, right, through his dream. His clothes adhere to his body with dried blood. Something close to him moves. His hand searches for the Remington. Is it loaded? Did he change cylinders? He springs up, scrambling along Valley Pike. His horse is gone, shot out from under him. Snow stumbles forward on foot. Behind him, soldiers lie stiff in mud and grass beside a road where they marched straight and strong the day before. Rumors of Union defeat at Front Royal rumble through the regiment as they march toward Winchester. All semblance of formation disappears with the first sniper fire. Grapeshot from artillery at Middletown encourages a near rout.

Jostled to the rear, he picks an Enfield off a headless soldier. Returning fire with it slows his progress. Distance to his regiment opens, as a sergeant yells orders. A whimpering boy stumbles along beside Snow. Then they march as one, the boy slumping against him. They push ahead into a pulsing, blue haze. It pushes back. The scene turns red and then gray. Snow's brother, David, gaunt in his dirty gray uniform, smiles through the fog of Snow's dream. David pours water over Snow's aching head. Snow floats through his dream on the ceiling of their shared childhood bedroom. In a dark cold night, David stands at the window. He reads the letter with "David" penned on the envelope. Uniformed in a gray shell jacket and kepi, he looks down the field to the pier jutting into Snows Run. A workboat waits to cross the Potomac, waits to return him to his cavalry regiment. David's breath frosts the window glass. The crushed pages twists in his grip. Draping his frock coat over his shoulders, he leaves through the closed door, stumbles over doorstops lying next to each other, and fades out of Snow's dream.

Snow woke standing by the bed, Colt revolver in hand. Dank air escaping through a gaps in the ancient tunnel's cover mixed with the sweet smell of roses, as a breeze lifted it out into the night. Two doorstops lay, one beside the other, against the bedroom door now slightly ajar. He was alone.

Snow sat on the bed and gingerly placed the Colt on the washstand. After rubbing his shoulder and right arm, he took several deep long breaths. Memories ticked in order through his mind; his rescue and exchange after the Battle of Winchester in May of '82, a long convalescence at Snow's Rest, rumors of David's capture at Antietam in September. Secretary of War Stanton's refusal to allow an exchange of commissioned officers left David to suffer untreated wounds at Point Lookout Prison.

Snow smiled now at the audacity of boys, for that is what they were. John, named Kojo as a boy, appeared with news of David's peril. Through a dark, moonless night, they paddled the single log canoe down St. Mary's River and into Potter's Creek. They dragged it through marshes behind Cornfield Point and into Point Lookout Creek above the prison. Laying low in the canoe, mired in freezing swamp and brambles, Snow and Kojo developed both a plan for David's rescue and the courage to execute it. Snow watched the sentries marching a perimeter around the fenceless prison camp. On a moonless night in January of '63, Snow waited until the patrolling sentries met and turned to march back. Behind their backs, he crawled across the clearing on elbows and knees into the camp. Hidden among the prisoners in cast off CSA rags, Snow ate meals and played cards until he could repeat the process in reverse. On the next clouded night, he crawled out with David on his back. In the freezing swamp, he called to Kojo with coded owl hoots. The canoe glided in silence from its camouflage. They slipped along the shoreline into Snow's Run and carried David down into the tunnel. Snow used John's childhood name for the last time. Soon, the three boys would separate in the gulf of war.

Two weeks passed before soldiers showed up at the Rest looking for David who lay hidden beneath the house. David's silence was broken only once when he asked for Ellen. Louisa Mae Cawsin, mother of Jane and Ellen, crept down the ladder and along the tunnel in her worn mourning clothes. She held David's hands in hers as they wept together. At great expense, the Cawsins had sent both daughters away to a Connecticut boarding school for the duration of the war. Tragically, Ellen had died during the first winter. One morning, David was gone. Snow returned to his own unit soon after.

Kojo disappeared. Years later, he returned as John Benjamin Lundy. A veteran of the 38th Regiment United States Colored Troops, he fought at Chaffins Farm along with his friend, Medal of Honor recipient James H. Harris. Snow and John never discussed the war.

The second time Snow woke, he lay pondering the dream, separating it from reality. The heat of the day was rising through the house, boards covered the tunnel tightly, and the bedroom door was latched again. The doorstops sat side by side against the bedroom door. After securing the Colt, Snow wandered down the stairs, through the central hall, and into the dining room. A plate of biscuits and pot of coffee sat under a towel on the sideboard. They were cold. He took them to the kitchen.

Voices from the backyard summer kitchen echoed through the kitchen screen door. The clear sharp chop of an ax rang out as Snow crossed through the back gardens. Through the summer kitchen, opened double doors, he observed John leaning against the kitchen wall. John smiled down at a stack of hoecakes under on the cast iron stove. Sarah deftly added another cake, pretending to slap away John's hand as he pretended to steal it. John grinned, pulling back in mock fright. Through a space in back wall slats, Snow saw Paul splitting firewood with a casual swing of ax. Paul spotted Snow and hesitated in his swing. John glanced up, his face serious. Smiling, Sarah took the cold coffee and biscuits. She dumped the cold coffee in a bucket and refilled the pot with a strong, hot brew. She handed Snow a tray with a pot of coffee, a tin coffee cup, and a plate of hot hoecakes with molasses.

Snow nodded. "Thank you, Sarah." To John, he added, "Later, we will walk the farm."

John nodded, "Yes, Mr. Snow."

Annoyed, Snow tried to remember the last time John addressed him as Mr. Snow. Breakfast tray in hand, he marched back to the house and let the back screen door slam. He walked through the house kitchen and down the hall to Jane's drawing room. His annoyance abated when he found two fresh rosebuds in a crystal vase on the piano. Silken petals caressed his fingers like the softness of Jane's face. Her presence hovered in the room, lifting his spirits. Echoes of her music wandered through his memory. Music sheets scattered across the stand above the open keys. One music sheet lay open on the bench. His annoyance returned.

"No one is allowed to play Jane's piano! No one is allowed to touch her music!" His voice echoed in the empty room, down the empty hall, through the empty house. One petal dropped from the rosebuds. Snow sat down at Jane's writing desk, ate his breakfast, and regained his composure.

Finally, he opened Jane's desk and removed a small cedar chest. Sorting through the letters, Snow compared them to the one he brought from Baltimore, the one signed "Lovingly, A" and dated April 1894. He had found the it quite by accident. His new Baltimore housekeeper was sorting Jane's clothes, and he happened to be in the room when the envelope fell from an old apron pocket. It skidded across the room and settled at his feet. Oddly, it weighed heavily in his hand as he picked it up. Snow sat to catch his breath before reading it. "A" thanked Jane for gifts of cloth and money. She was coming for a visit to Snows Rest in June and bringing "our little one". No other letters from "A" were found among Jane's carefully organized correspondence. Snow searched Jane's desk for other envelopes addressed in the same handwriting or any dating back as far 1894. The heat of day brought out cicadas to sing an early lament complementing Snow's darkening mood.

Snow abandoned the search and set about writing two letters. The first, to the Sisters Overzee, enquired about the mantle clock. He placed this in his pocket. The second, to third cousin Enoch Snow who lived across St. Mary's River, invited him for rye whiskey and business in the evening.

Blotting the second letter, he looked through the long drawing-room windows and spotted a small catboat grounded several feet from the dock. A woman rocked the little boat to no avail. By the time Snow ran half way down the hill, a skipjack from the river was closing in. An exceptionally tall, young waterman stepped into the shallows. After rocking Carrie

Darberry's catboat free, he guided it to a piling and tied it. He had little difficulty lifting Carrie and her basket up to the walkway. Watching this brawny performance of chivalry, Snow wondered what he could possibly have done alone to free her.

"Thank you so much." Snow managed to gasp as he reached them. Noticing the younger man's tattered clothes, Snow scanned the makeshift collection of gear on skipjack with an odd orange and black waterline. "Let me show my gratitude." But, the waterman turned away in red-faced annoyance.

"And ask one more favor. May I interest you in delivering a letter to Solomon's Island and returning with the answer tomorrow? The recipients will gladly put you up for the night. I'm William Snow." Snow offered his hand.

"Josiah Jenks, Judge." The waterman shook hands, eyeing the letter and proffered cash. "Solomons would lose me two, maybe three days crabbin'. Dependin on weather. Need my brother, Buddy, along to sail the Bee Bea a day and a night if I'm to get your reply here tomorrow."

Bartering continued until Josiah Jenks agreed to deliver the correspondence if Snow doubled the amount offered. Snow added the cost of room and board at the Overzee, for the Sisters sake. With negotiations finalized, Jenks sailed away, the Sister's letter tucked in the bib of his overalls. Later, Snow would wonder if his impulsiveness had been good judgment or good luck.

Snow turned to greet Carrie Darberry, who smiled amusedly. Snow smiled back and offered his arm for the long walk up the hill.

"Mrs. Darberry, welcome to Snow's Rest. It is good to see you again. I suspect I have learned something about striking a bargain today."

"I should hope so." Carrie replied with one eyebrow raised.

Snow resumed, "Let us stroll up to the Rest and have some refreshments." They walked up the road discussing yesterday's sail down to St. Mary's, comfortable in each other's company. Two figures stood on the hilltop. Sarah disappeared toward the kitchen. Paul waited until the Jenks' skipjack sailed out of Snows Run before he started down the hill.

Removing his hat, Paul began with, "Good morning, Mrs. Darberry, Judge Snow. Judge, is there anything I can do to help you?"

"No, Paul. We're fine."

"Judge, if you need anything delivered, I am at your disposal."

"Now that you mention it, Paul, I do have a letter to my cousin, Enoch. It's on the drawing room desk, and needs to be delivered this morning."

"I will deliver it immediately." Paul

retrieved the envelope from the drawing room and removed his hat as he trotted past them on his way to the dock.

When they reached the shaded veranda, Snow and Carrie paused to watch Paul scull the small flat-bottomed dory out of the run. His skill with the craft confirmed his deep county roots, in contrast to the vocabulary and polish acquired during a year at Morgan State. Jane Cawsin Snow had sent Paul Lundy, her piano protégé to school, hoping he would return a revered clergyman. Instead, Paul had clung to his love of music. Gazing after him, Snow felt something crawl on the back of his neck, followed by a chilling sting prickling down his arm. Brushing his shirtsleeve, he expected to find a bee or spider. Instead, his hand came away with a rose petal.

"Perhaps I should have asked Paul to return with an answer." He spoke absently, more to himself than to Carrie as he held the door for her.

"We only get what we ask for, and sometimes not even that." She patted his arm.

As they crossed the foyer, Carrie looked around remembering. Her eyes came to rest on the front room mantel clock. Sarah brought a tea tray arranged to Jane's dictates. A pot of tea sat beside strawberry rhubarb tarts on Jane's blue and white china. The two rosebuds in a ceramic bud vase, one for each child lost at birth, were sweet and sad. Snow sat to the left on the sofa as if leaving room for Jane. Carrie sat opposite Snow in a Morris chair. Snow thanked Sarah and remarked how Jane would be pleased. He drifted in memories of Jane entertaining her guests with this same ritual. Turning the bud vase gently around, he came out of his reminiscence with, "Welcome to Snow's Rest Mrs. Darberry. It's good to see you. You are my first guest this summer." Carrie poured tea and waited as Sarah's footsteps faded through the back of the house.

"I came today to pay my respects, and visit Jane's grave. Also, I have a gift of strawberry jam Ellen Mae and I put up in June." From her basket, Carrie removed a wax topped jar of preserves and a bouquet of mixed wildflowers wrapped in a wet tea towel. "Richard and I were pleased when you decided to bring Jane home to the Rest. We are hoping your stay will last the summer, so we may exchange visits often." Her sincerity and warmth shown like a beam of light into the dark of Snow's grief.

"Thank you very much, Carrie. May I call you Carrie?" She smiled and nodded. Snow continued, "These preserves will be delightful on our breakfast toast. And, the flowers are lovely. When we finish our refreshments, we can visit the garden."

With his offer of more tea declined, they strolled to the garden with the flowers. She held his arm, and they viewed the family graves.

"I know the family calls you Snow, but I would rather call you William, if you don't mind."

"Yes, it would be fine. Jane called me William.   David was named after my mother's father who had no sons. I am named after my own father, but my hair was almost white as a child and looked like snow.   Hence   the   name.   Childhood nicknames can stick like clay after a spring rain."

Carrie smiled.   "It is touching your family has a memorial to David. Do you have any idea where he is buried?"

"Actually, we are not certain. At the beginning, David fought in the First Maryland Cavalry, Army of Northern Virginia. In 1862, he rescued me after the Battle of Front Royal, and John brought me home across the river. Later, David was assigned to the Third Brigade of the

Cavalry Corps, Army of Northern Virginia. His name disappeared from CSA rosters after the Chancellorsville Campaign." The usual unease swept over Snow with the uncertainties of this recitation.

Distancing himself from his discomfort, Snow led Carrie into the rose garden. Roses bloomed wildly, no longer pampered by Jane's love and dedication. Snow reflected how quickly the passage of time erased human efforts. Carrie read the inscription "William Thomas Snow III b. July 4, 1844", and "Jane Louisa Cawsin Snow b. July 5, 1846, d. October 28, 1902". She placed her bouquet between two white marble cherubs and made the sign of the cross. They stood in silent prayer for several minutes.

"When Bud died it was so sudden, no chance to say goodbye." Carrie reflected. "So unexpected, I kept thinking I heard his wagon creak in the yard for months after." Snow turned to Carrie, his own grief welling up. Far behind her, he saw a skipjack with a black and yellow waterline making careful progress back into the run. The moment passed, and Carrie turned to follow his gaze.

"Richard has something to tell you." She sighed, looking down as they strolled to the house. A man disembarked at the dock, and the skipjack sailed out of Snows Run.

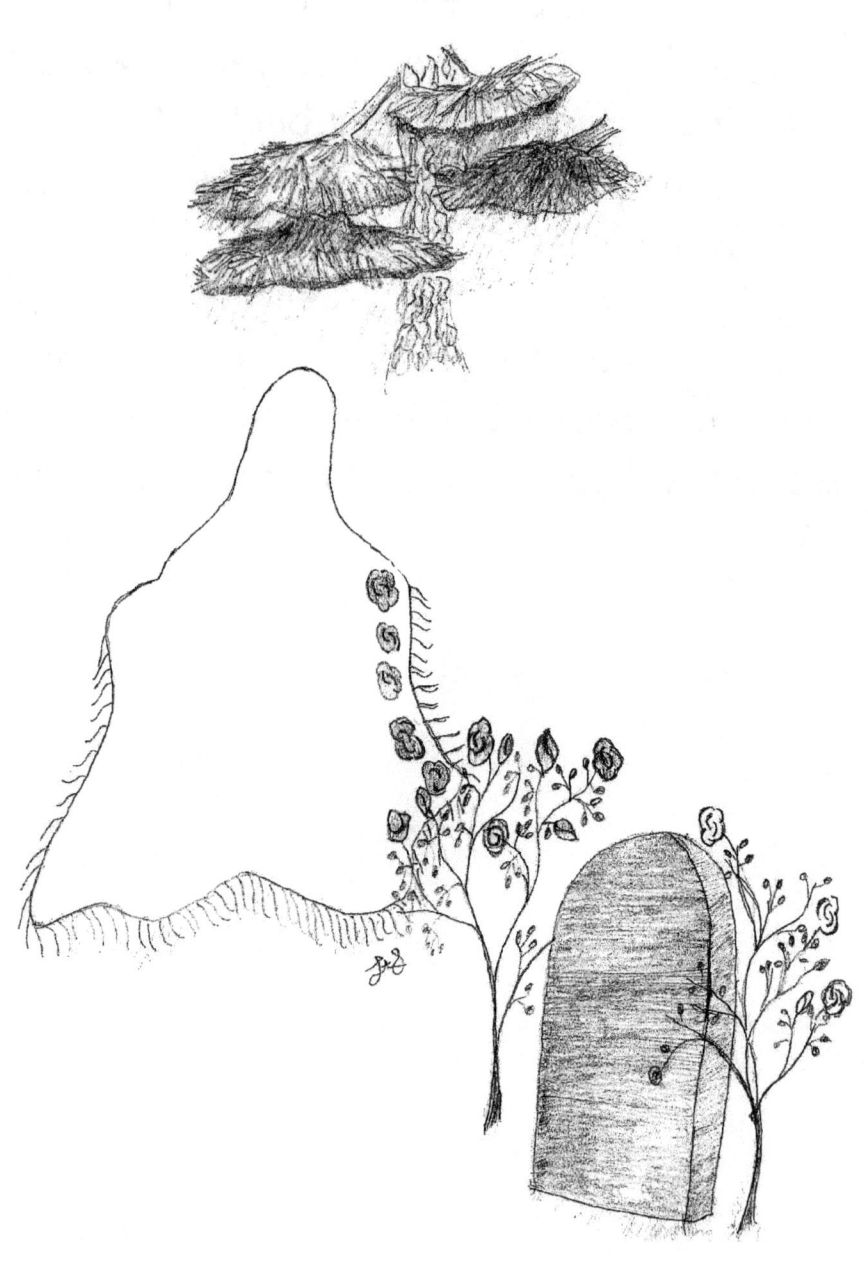

Chapter 7 Revelations

Ah, sunshine may fade
From the heavens above,
No twilight have we
To the day of our love.
        Paul Lawrence Dunbar 1872 - 1906

Snow raised his hand in greeting to the man striding up from the dock. Richard ducked his head, hid his face beneath the brim of a farmer's straw hat, and did not wave. Watching Richard continue up the hill with a determined gait, Snow guided Carrie back into the Rest and closed the front double doors. By the time Richard reached the porch, Snow and Carrie sat quietly waiting in the front room. The knocker banged down hard several times. Snow took his time getting to the left side door. He opened it leaving his right hand free.   Startled, Richard had to step sideways into the open doorway.

"Good afternoon Mr. Darberry." Snow blocked the entrance until Richard removed his hat.

"Good afternoon, Judge." Richard shifted his weight back and forth. "I am looking for my mother. I hailed the Jenks brothers on their weekly run to Solomon's, and they agreed to bring me here." Snow smiled at himself. A skirt rustled as Carrie shifted in the chair behind him. Snow stepped aside. The younger man gave the foyer and front room a searching glance. His hat brim twisted in his hands as he nodded to Carrie.

"Is Hattie with you, Mother?" The son failed to see Snow's look of surprise. The mother did not meet Snow's eyes or answer Richard.

Once inside, Richard continued with, "When I got up this morning, you were both gone. If she isn't here with you, where did she go?"

"After last night, I'm surprised to see either of you up before noon." Carrie retorted.

Richard blushed. "I searched around the house and barns, but there's no sign of Hattie. I'm concerned for her safety."

Carrie interrupted. "Hattie knows everyone along the river from her days at St. Mary's Female Seminary. I'm sure she will be just fine."

While the hat spun in his grip, Richard ignored his mother. He continued speaking to Snow. "Annie Clarke came to the Elms after Ellen Mae's funeral. She insisted Hattie and Carrie move out immediately. James took Annie's side in the matter. Hattie had nowhere to go, so we took her with us." Glancing at Carrie, he added, "...until she can find a position."

Sarah appeared with a lunch tray of sandwiches, dried fruit, Smith Island cake, and coffee, sparking Snow's appetite. Richard stood a few minutes resisting the delayed departure. He checked the time on the mantle clock. Finally, he surrendered to his hunger and sat down. The three ate quietly for several minutes.

"You took Hattie Wells in when she has nowhere to turn. You were exceptionally kind." Snow directed his comment to Carrie, who looked away stiffly without reply.

Richard answered, "We are especially fond of Hattie and keep her under our special guidance and protection." Snow watched a pinched expression flash across Carrie's face as Richard continued. "Hattie suffered a terrible shock when Thomas left for the cavalry. Mother sent her to St. Mary's Female Seminary to help Hattie put away her past. After Hattie received her Certificate of Graduation, she became Ellen Mae's personal secretary. I gave her experience taking dictation and writing legal documents in my office. She aspires to become a secretary with a law firm in

Baltimore. When Ellen Mae and Hattie visited Mrs. Snow last October, Hattie hoped to gain your support for her aspirations." There was a questioning tone in Richard's remark. Snow was having trouble remembering the visit, thinking it must have been before Jane died. Examining reflections in his coffee, Snow remembered. He remembered how vibrant Jane Cawsin Snow was that morning. He remembered returning from court late in the afternoon. He remembered that moment, the moment he knew. She was so still. Jane was not just napping on the chaise. He stirred his coffee.

Snow refocused on his guests who were peering back. "Will James Abbott inherit a complete interest in the Coode Yard through the death of his wife? Did Ellen Mae leave anything to Thomas, Hattie, or Carrie?"

Mother and son exchanged glances. "Ellen left Hattie a small amount. She left nothing to Mother. Mother continued to live at the Elms under the terms of Old Benjamin's will, but Ellen Mae made no provision. It does state I may continue to use my office at the yard. She left Old Benjamin's clock to Thomas. The clock is missing. She also left Thomas a sealed letter, which I gave to him after the funeral. Otherwise, Thomas inherits nothing unless..." Richard's voice trailed. He checked the time giving the clock a lingering stare.

Carrie prompted. "It's better if you explain. I might get the details confused." Her son sighed with resignation.

"Thomas may not know this, yet." He glanced at the mantle clock again.

"Thomas doesn't know this, yet. It is possible... There is some evidence James Lathmore Abbott..." Snow remembered James Abbott guiding Annie Clarke down the church aisle during the funeral, his hand at the small of her back. A sudden insight flashed through his thoughts. Questions whirled, but he let Richard tell the story.

Impatient, Carrie directed Richard's recitation. "Start with the argument between Ellen Mae and James just before Mrs. Snow's funeral October last."

Richard hadn't taken his eyes off the clock. "Is that clock identical to the one in Old Benjamin's study?"

Snow scrutinized the clock. "I don't recall seeing a clock in Ben Coode's study." Carrie peered into her coffee cup.

Richard leaned forward and quietly began. "About a year after Ellen Mae and James married, Old Ben gave James permission to bring his sister, Annie Clarke, and her family. They lived in a small house behind Coode Yard. There is a boy, Jeremiah, and Annie's husband, Arthur. Arthur has a head injury. Jeremiah was about three when they moved into the house. When the boy got older, I befriended him, took him fishing, and bought him books. One day, when I asked after his father, Jeremiah yelled at me, claimed Arthur wasn't his father. Well, I was surprised. I tried to talk to James about it, as James is his uncle. I think Jeremiah was about ten at the time. James went to the Clark's cottage. I could hear him yelling at Annie and Jeremiah. That same day James moved Annie Clarke and her family across Back Creek into another house, deep in the woods and out of sight. Before she left, Annie came to my office. She was shaking when she told me I was never to take Jeremiah fishing or talk to him again."

"That's not what Ellen Mae and James Abbott fought about." Carrie interrupted.

The son acquiesced. "When Mrs. Snow died, Ellen Mae asked me to escort her to the funeral. She said James couldn't leave the boatyard, which I thought was strange."

Carrie interrupted. "They had an argument about that. It was the first time I heard them raise voices to each other in years. Not because they always got along, mind you. They rarely spoke to each other at all. James Lathmore Abbott had relatives in Baltimore. Ellen Mae had never met them. She wanted James to accompany her to Jane's funeral and then visit his relations. He said the Lathmores had insulted his sister, and he would never speak to them again. Then he made excuses about not leaving the boatyard."

"How did you come by that clock?" Richard staring at it.

"Richard, until you told me just now, I didn't know it might come from the Elms. It was sent to me." Both Richard and Carrie gave him questioning looks. "Please finish what you have to tell me about James Abbott. Then, you can help me solve the mystery of the clock."

Richard shifted in his chair, pushing

back from the tea table. He paused for a long minute, contemplating the clock. "Last October, after Mrs. Snow's funeral, I tried unsuccessfully to find James Abbott's Baltimore relatives. So, I hired a Pinkerton agent to search for them. The agent found one Lathmore family in Carroll County who knew a James Wells Abbott whose grandmother had been a Lathmore. They thought he lived with his wife somewhere in West Virginia."

"Did you tell Ellen Mae?", Snow queried.

"No. I thought about it all through Advent and Christmas. In February, I paid the agent to search the census records at the Commerce Department in Washington. In the 1890 federal census, the agent found a James L. Abbott living in the Cabin Creek District of Kanawha County, West Virginia. He had a wife, Ann. The agent couldn't find them in the 1900 census." Carrie was almost in tears.

"And you didn't you tell Ellen Mae?"

Snow, surprised at Richard's diligent search, was astonished at his silence.

"No. There was a chance another James Abbott had married a wife named Ann. Census records show many repeated family names, like my own for example. There are three cousins in my family, all named Richard Darberry, with only middle names to tell us apart. Your cousin Enoch named his second son William David Snow. If I told Ellen, and I was wrong..."

"But, she knew anyway," Carrie whispered softly.

"Mother, it is not possible." Richard's arrogant dismissal made Carrie turn her face away, placing a napkin over her mouth. Focused out the front room window, down the hill and across the River, she seemed in a far distant place. Snow marveled Richard had shared the Pinkerton Agency report with Carrie, or had he?

"Did you have a written report from the agent? Could Ellen Mae have found it?"

Snow's mind grasped possible consequences.

Richard shook his head no. "There are letters and the census report. In April, I advanced the agent a sum for travel to Cabin Creek. He had a copy of Ellen and James's wedding photograph with him. His final report hasn't arrived yet. I kept all the Pinkerton correspondence in Old Benjamin's strongbox at my office under lock and key. No one else has access." Snow caught the flash of disbelief crossing Carrie's face.

Carrie interrupted, her voice quivering. "The morning Ellen Mae died, I was dusting the upstairs parlor. Hattie was at Ellen's desk in the study. She came into the parlor all flustered, a letter in her hand. She pulled the letter to herself real quick when she saw me. Gave me a sharp look. I asked her what was wrong. She just went down to the kitchen."

Drop-jawed, Richard stared at his

mother in amazement. Snow couldn't decide if he was more surprised at Carrie's story or at Richard's ignorance of it.

Carrie continued. "After a few minutes, I heard raised voices. Ellen said something like 'After all I have done for you'. Then there was silence. Hattie left the house. The back screen door banged shut hard. I looked out the window. Hattie took the back path along the windbreak to the boatyard. Later, Ellen Mae was dead." Carrie's coffee cup rattled in the saucer.

"How much later?" Snow asked abruptly while contemplating Richard's wary expression.

Abruptly, Richard put his arm around the weeping Carrie, and interrupted with, "I had better take my mother home." He lifted her from the chair before she could answer Snow.

Snow followed them to the front porch where Richard vehemently insisted on walking Carrie to the dock alone. Part way down the hill, Carrie slumped and Richard lifted her in his arms. Snow started down the hill, but Richard had placed Carrie in her little catboat and cast off before Snow reached them. The lone sail barely filled as the little craft drifted into the river. Richard used a pole to hold the sail out from the hull in hopes of catching a breeze and sculled the craft forward with the rudder. With humid mist hanging like fog over land and water, the little boat faded to a blur along with Richard's concerns for Hattie's whereabouts.

Back in the drawing room, Snow sat in contemplation. After some time, he continued his search of Jane's correspondence. He gathered the dated, ribbon wrapped packets back into the small cedar chest and retreated to the cooler back screened porch. At its rear, Snow's Rest backed up on a stand of old growth pines and oaks, many as large as king's trees. Three men could not join hands around some of the oaks. The pines scented the afternoon breeze. Borders of yellow Tansy bloomed among the English boxwoods around the porch, discouraging flies and mosquitoes. A rose embroidered, cream shawl lay across Jane's old wooden rocker. He gathered the shawl to his face. Phrases of love and sorrow, family jokes and anecdotes waited in the lingering familiar scent. Pins and needles crept down his arm, numbing his fingers. Gently, lovingly, he placed the shawl back over the rocker's arms. Then, he read the letters for clues surmising what Jane wrote from the responses of others.

Songs of cicadas turned to the chorus of tree frogs. Sarah, looking tired, appeared with a supper tray of refried biscuits, sliced cold chicken, and tomatoes. Snow remembered Sarah as barely more than a girl when John finally married at 42 years of age.

"Thank you, Sarah." She nodded. Snow

gathered the letters back into the chest, leaving it on the rocker. Back in the front room, he added his prized bottle of rye whiskey with four glasses to the tray. On the front porch, he lit torches of cedar oil mixed with tansy and sassafras root, his own recipe for avoiding insects. As the sun set behind rumbling clouds, Snow ate his supper, sipped his whiskey and waited.

Evening commenced with a cooling breeze that kept the voracious mosquitoes at bay. The supper was satisfying. The whiskey, a Melrose Rye, Goldsborough's blend of five whiskeys aged for six months, went down smoothly. Cousin Enoch failed to sail down the St. Mary's River. At one point, Snow thought he saw John watching in darkness just beyond the reach of torch light. Snow poured a second glass of Melrose and raised it in invitation. The vision melted away.

A milk-white moon wandered across the sky, its pale reflection like a corpse floating on the quiet river. Melancholy howls of distant, chorusing red wolves drifted through the night in mournful greeting. Overcome with need for Jane's company, Snow wandered to the garden. An aromatic mix of boxwoods, pine, and roses filled his head. Something soft as wings of a moth brushed his face. Wrapped in the cream shawl, she floated among the roses, an illusion of grace above her own grave. Attributing Jane's apparition to the Melrose, Snow took a deep breath and shook his head. Jane glided to obscurity in dark, stately oaks and pines.

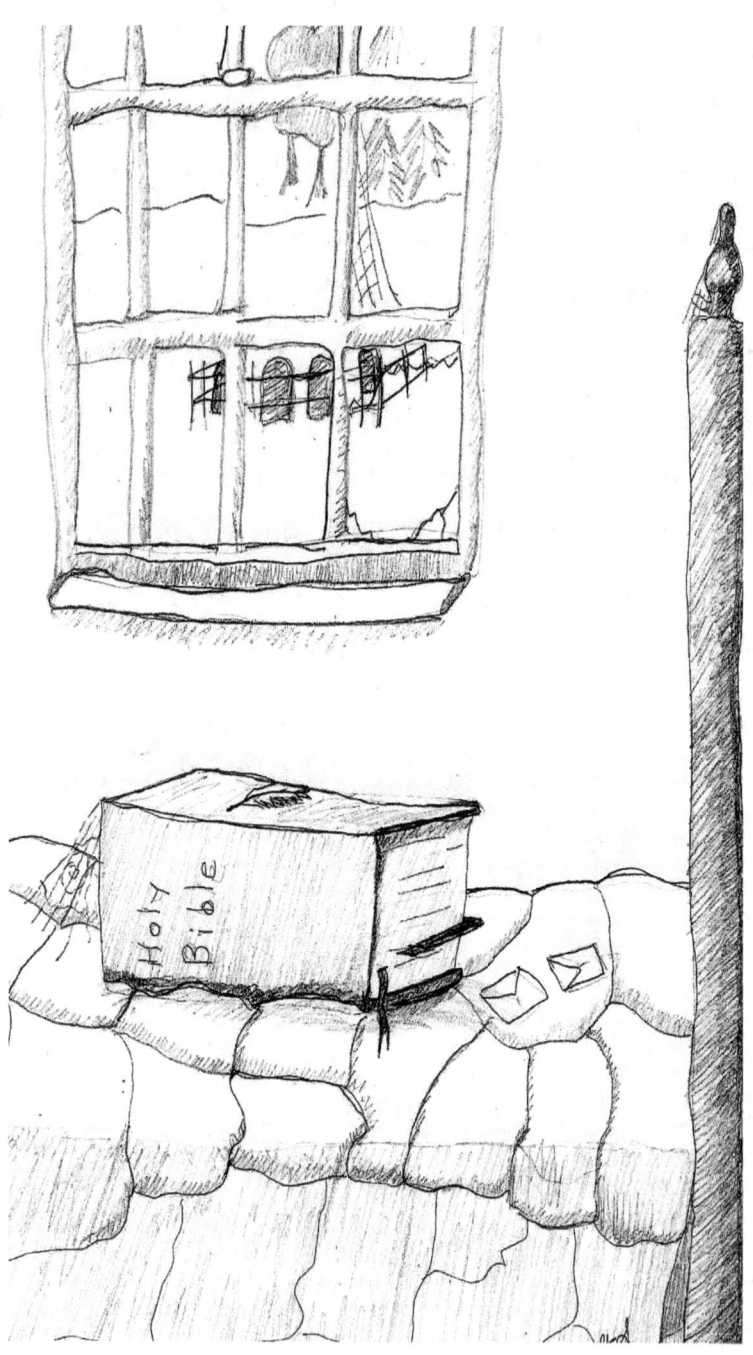

Chapter 8: Cawsin Farm

To be ignorant of the past is to forever be a child.
  Marcus Tullius Cicero, 106 – 43 BCE

A young and strong John carried the wounded Snow up the stairs. A dream of the memory jolted Snow awake. Predawn shadows lay softly over the room calming him until his mind cleared. Then he remembered Paul had carried him up the stairs. Snow recalled the scent of roses and a cream shawl floating into the darkness of the pines.

As light fingered its way into the room, Snow descended stealthily into the tunnel. In the hiding place, his hands moved over the bill of sale and into the embroidered purse. His thumb rifled the bills. Behind the tunnel wall behind the front room wood closet, Snow heard John's muffled voice calling to Sarah. John's voice filled with gentleness whenever he called to his wife. She answered from a distance perhaps from the summer kitchen. Creeping back up the ladder, Snow cast off his suspicions in the unfolding morning light. A change of clothes, clean linens, and a fresh pitcher of water waited on the washstand.

Ready for the day, Snow hesitated before descended the main staircase to the shaded, front porch. Sarah appeared with strong black coffee and plain toast. An aromatic bitterness in the coffee revealed the presence of willow bark meant to relieve Snow's impending headache. Rays of sun peered over trees into the faces of daisies and scattered day over the fields. Bees bumbled their way through stalks of Queen Anne's lace along the south side of the porch. Finished with his coffee, Snow rose and walked through the Rest to the back porch. The shawl and letters were gone.

Across the yard, an overgrown path

wound into the woods. By the opening three white-tailed deer foraged as somewhere in the woods their fawns dozed in shadows. One doe surveyed the yard, her huge ears hearing his every move, his every breath. Casually she moved down the path. The others followed slipping among trees in silence. In the safety of shadows, they nibbled on leaf buds along the path.

Recalling the previous night's wolf howls, Snow retrieved his Colt. In Jane's drawing room, he pocketed the Baltimore letter that still lay in her opened desk. With the holster and belt slung over his shoulder, he crossed the yard and slipped into the woods.

The deer had paused at a turn in the path. Here, the largest oak on Snows Rest was marked high on its trunk with a broad arrow claiming it for King George. As boys, Snow and David climbed the lofty trunk to trace the mark. Even then, the slight scar in the bark was scarcely detectable. The lead doe took two cautious steps off the path into shadows. First lowering her head, she peered into the underbrush. Abruptly, she stomped a hoof in warning, whistled through her nostrils, bolted, and was gone. White tails flashed and vanished into the trees. Snow waited. The crashing receded. Blue jays filled the trees with rakish calls. Crows moved in sending the jays down the path.

Snow moved along to where the path crossed a dark red, leaf-clogged trickle of a creek. Fallen logs once made a bridge here. Once, a pile of old bricks made a secret place where Cawsin girls left letters for Snow boys who left replies.

A moment came to him perhaps it was April with dogwoods. Jane ran down the path, skirts lifted. From forest shadows, his eyes drank up her graceful feet and the outline of strong thighs through a summer dress. Like a wolf of fairytales, he jumped from hiding, growled, and laughed. She giggled and screamed in mock fear. They walked. They talked. He watched her face change with each word until she fell silent into a stolen kiss.

Snow stepped across the creek. A weathered back corner of the Cawsin farmhouse peered down the trail from a clearing. Tall grass, scrub pines, and the skeletal remains of a giant fallen oak filled the backyard. As he walked up the path, a partly demolished summer kitchen peered from under the fallen tree. He stared into the ruins. A veil lifted from a long ago lurid memory. One night, spying as little brothers do, curiosity led a young Snow to follow David here. Memories of watching tangled legs and hearing cries of pleasure in the darkness came back. He walked wide around the devastation and searched the vacant windows of the abandoned farmhouse ahead. One grey, silent cloud roiled over the pines, the advance scout of an afternoon offensive. Heavy stillness in humid air leached power from soft rumbles of an approaching storm.

A yawning maw opened in the house where double back doors once kept the world out. Inside, disturbances over the dusty kitchen floor showed multiple visitors, some human. Beyond, an even layer of dust settled unmarked everywhere. Snow cleared his throat and stretched the tension out of his back. Late morning air sighed through the stifled rooms as his footfalls echoed on the stairs.

Through an upstairs window, Snow looked out over the Cawsin family graveyard. Jane's ancestors lay under stone tablets within a rusted broken fence. A marble memorial to Jane's sister, Ellen Frances Cawsin, glistened white among the grey slate and sandstone markers. Snow recalled the inscription, "She is loved and loves the loving one, and dreams while sleeping he is near." Untended pink roses grew around it. Beyond the rusted iron fencing, rows of regular indentations still held a few markers of burials before the War of the Rebellion. All her life, Jane tended the graves of her grandparents, her parents, and Ellen's memorial. Ellen, who loved David, had died in Jane's arms far away. Cawsin ancestors held this farm firmly in their cold, eternal grip.

Thoughts of his own ancestors turned Snow to his task. Not expecting to find Jane's missing letters under the undisturbed dust, he still thought he might find something. Something here might lead him to identify "Lovingly, A" and "our little one". Two large bedrooms occupied the entire second floor. Empty of furnishings, the children's room viewed opened sky. The horsehair plaster ceiling had collapsed under the weight of invading rain through a damaged roof. Swallows chirped, and flickered in and out, attending mud dabbed nests in the attic rafters.

The master bedroom was intact and furnished. Dust covered linens spread neatly across the bed. Towels hung evenly on the washstand. A dressing gown hung on a peg inside the open wardrobe door as if the owner had just dressed and gone down to breakfast. Hesitating on the threshold, Snow focused on a small roll top writing desk by a window. He stepped gently across the room as layers of dust billowing around his feet.

Ancient ribbons bound brittle, yellowed letters that crumbled under his touch. Pages dangled in pieces along torn folds. Snow sorted through letters written to *Louisa Mae* Cawsin, Jane's mother. He sorted by signature, and then by date. As he read, shadows of late afternoon crept from under Cawsin gravestones marking the passage of time. He read letters from Annabelle last. A was for Annabelle. Snow's mind rebelled against the first reference to Papa. One dated April 1885, revealing Papa's death, posted from Weatherford County, Texas. Another letter written in 1886, said Annabel and her husband, Luther Wells, would move to her in-laws in Kanawha County, West Virginia. She would continue to write. Another letter written in 1888 said Annabel would come with "my little one" in June.

Snow touched his pocket containing Jane's Baltimore letter. At what point did she know? She must have known, must have known for years. A sharp pain radiated across his back. Snow scattered letters off the desk slamming down the roll top. The echo of his anger sent crescendos of swallows out the open attic roof. A few escaped chirping into the house. A single swallow arrived behind him on the bed. Snow turned to see it perched on two large books, rose petals in its beak. Dropping the wilted petals, it disappeared, a thrashing of feathers through a broken windowpane.   Dust drifted across the bedcovers as Snow reached for the books. The huge, two-volume family bible sank deeply into the feather mattress. Volume I, printed in 1825, contained records of Cawsin births, marriages, and deaths. Entries in various hands occupied the last blank pages. They were faded by date. His finger slid down to the latest entries where he found his name beside Jane's with the date of their wedding. He found Ellen's name, alone, with dates of birth and death. No name connected beside Ellen's name, but a blank line descended from it containing the word child. The corner of a tintype photograph protruded from Volume II. Gingerly, he slid it out. Snow looked into the eyes of an older David seated for a family portrait, cane in hand. A dark haired child, about 4 years of age, stood beside him, her head barely up to David's waist. A woman Snow recognized as Ellen's maid, Addie from Cawsin Farm, stood behind them with an infant in her arms. Snow turned over the photo and read "David Horatio Snow, Annabelle Cawsin Snow, Addie Cawsin and child". His arm swept across the bed crashing both volumes into the wall. Tightness in his chest forced Snow to sit and gasp for breath.

Eventually, he retrieved the letters from the desk, slipped them and the photograph into his buttoned shirt, and stepped slowly down the stairs. He shuffled across the yard and paused by the crumbling summer kitchen. A collapsed wall revealed mosquito netting hanging from the rafters to shelter faded rag quilts that covered straw bedding strewn across the brick floor. An indigo blue linen jacket lay carefully folded over a worn carpetbag. Looking closer, Snow spotted an envelope next to the bag. He retrieved the unopened letter to his cousin Enoch.

Snow paused at the path through the

woods and turned to look back at the wreckage of Cawsin Farm. Storm clouds, advancing across the river, released an afternoon deluge. At the bend in the woods, three buzzards sat sentinel in a pine beside the king's oak, hunchbacked against the torrent. Trees thrashed like drowning swimmers in a violent current, and broken boughs crashed to the forest floor behind him. Snow picked up his pace to a trot in the mud and slipped. Recovering, he stumbled on. At the Rest's back porch, he sank into a wicker chair and stared back down the path. He had caught his breath by the time he realized his Colt's holster weight was light.

Snows Rest, A Maryland Mystery

L. A. Stewart

Chapter 9 Missing

They who travel far easily miss their way.
Sir Henry Wotton, 1568-1639

Snow's hands had stopped shaking by the time John and Sarah found him. Sarah coaxed him into the front room under John's silent scrutiny of the empty holster.

Sarah began with "You sit here. I'll get something cool to..." Snow held up the faded tintype. Sarah took a step back and wiped her already dry hands on her apron. John's expression went blank.

Unuttered accusations hung in the air like motionless hands of a clock all run down. At length, a look of relief swept over John's face. He looked past Snow out the front room windows towards Snows Run.

"Got company." John exhaled the phrase. A moment passed before Snow

148

grasped his meaning and turned to look down the hill towards the Run. A gaff-rigged sloop, long at the waterline, drifted to the pier. Her sole occupant stepped off, looping the bow line around a piling. When the occupant reached half way up the hill, a skipjack, distinguished by its orange and black striped waterline, tacked into the Run under full sail. Sarah and John slipped away.

From behind the front room drapes, Snow scrutinized the man. A straw boater, shading his face, did little to conceal his intensity of purpose. A dust-covered laborer's shirt hanging loose did little to conceal the bulk strapped beneath. Determination partly disguised the man's limp. After removing the rosewood mantle clock to the dining room buffet, Snow waited until the brass knocker rapped a second time. He opened the left side of the double oak doors, leaving his right hand free. Thomas stood stern faced in the doorway. The hot and humid day left him damp and soiled.

"Thomas Coode, I hardly recognized you out of uniform. Good afternoon. Come in, come in." Snow's cheerful decorum and welcoming handshake guided Thomas into the foyer. Snow closed the door.

"Good afternoon, Judge." Thomas' glance shifted across the foyer, through the front room, down the hall. "It is good to see you again. I am here...."

Turning his back, Snow walked to the farthest chair in the front room and sat facing the windows. He gestured to the chair opposite. "Come in, Thomas. Please sit. It's not often an old man out here in God's country enjoys the pleasure of a guest."

After removing the straw boater, Thomas moved to the chair. He sat gingerly on the chair's edge, leaning forward.

"Unfortunately, my visit will be brief. I

have business with Carrie and Richard. I only stopped at the Rest to retrieve my clock. The Sisters sent it to you by mistake." Thomas started up from his chair at voices on the front porch.

Snow calmly went to the door, opening it before the Jenks brothers raised the knocker. Josiah Jenks stood alone at the door.

"Come in, Josiah. So good of you to come back on the next tide. I insist you come in, set yourself down, and rest awhile." Josiah raised an eyebrow and nodded. Standing tall, he stepped into the foyer. His searching gaze rested on Thomas as he followed Snow into the front room. He remained standing until Thomas sat down again.

"Well, Josiah, did you bring an answer to my letter?"

"Yes, we..., I did." Jenks handed Snow the letter. "Some interesting goins on up Solomon's way. Constable Stump had a talk with us. Wants you to know about them." Jenks sat upright, hands on his knees, his weight on the ball of his right foot. With his eyes on Thomas, he waited.

Thomas shifted in his chair and sat back. "Yes, well, I was starting to tell Judge Snow." He looked at the floor and worked the straw boater in a circle bending the brim. "A Pinkerton agent showed up at the Elms, looking for Richard. He had a report on an investigation of James Abbott. The investigation took him all the way to West Virginia. After learning of Ellen Mae's death, he gave the report to Constable Stump. Stump told me what's in the report."

Thomas paused looking directly at Snow. "It amazes me how things went on right in front of me, and I didn't see them."

Snow raised his eyebrows and gave Thomas a knowing nod. "Thomas, just tell me what you found out."

"Annie Clarke is not James Abbott's

sister.   She is actually his wife, and Jeremiah is his son.   Arthur Clarke is a brother Annie took in after Clarke sustained a head injury from a boating accident. As far as we can tell, James and Annie are still married.   So, Ellen Mae's marriage to James was not legal."

Snow showed no surprise.   "Can the agent prove this?   What does James Abbott say for himself?"

"I told James to move out of the Elms. At first, he refused.   Stump had a talk with him after looking over the Pinkerton agent's report. The agent had a notarized copy of James' and Annie's marriage certificate.   The Abbotts moved across Back Creek to Annie's house.   Stump thinks the agent's report and Ellen Mae's death cast suspicion on James Abbott. James stood to lose everything if Ellen Mae found out."

"So, Thomas, do you think Ellen Mae knew? If the agent's report is only now coming to light..."

"James claims Ellen Mae already lay on the kitchen floor when he arrived at the house around noon. He says Carrie stood at the bottom of the kitchen stairs when he entered through the back porch. James says Richard and Hattie arrived just behind him. I've come down to St. Mary's to ask Carrie if James is telling the truth." Thomas stopped. Snow let the pause widen between them.

"There's more." Josiah slid into the pause. "A waterman, Bib Pepys, had business with Abbott that morning. When Bib tied up to Coode Yard dock, he saw Hattie Wells runin' up the sail loft back stairs. Richard Darberry has an office there."

Snow frowned. "Is this the same waterman who told James Abbott about land agents on Coode land?" Jenks nodded. Turning to Thomas, Snow added, "And you're going to the Darberry farm alone?"

"No, your honor, he's not." Josiah replied staring firmly at Thomas. "Nonsense up Solomon's way ain't goin' spill over down here."

The center hall floorboards creaked. John slipped into Snow's view. A taller shadow fell across John into the foyer. From the seclusion of the dining room, the mantel clock struck the hour, and Thomas started up straight in his chair.

Ignoring Jenks, Thomas starred squarely into Snow's eyes. "My purpose here is to retrieve my grandfather's clock which is rightfully mine. My purpose at Darberry Farm is to learn if James Abbott is telling the truth."

Snow stared evenly back. "From your priorities, Thomas, it would seem the clock's importance exceeds the truth about Ellen Mae's death."

Slumped in his chair, Thomas contemplated Snow for a long moment. "Hattie meant me to have it. Early on the morning of Ellen Mae's funeral, she brought it from the Elms to put in my usual room at the Overzee Inn. Then the Sisters gave me a different room and let you stay in the larger, cooler one. That's why the Sisters thought the clock belonged to you when they found it."

"And the clock is important because...." Snow let the sentence float between them.

"Old Benjamin hid money in the thing, and he let Hattie wind it when she was little. So, she knew money probably hid there. Hattie wanted us to leave, to make a new life somewhere else, maybe Pennsylvania or New York. Well, it doesn't matter anymore."

"Instead, you broke the engagement and her heart. Then, the clock sat out of reach on the mantle in my room. I slept in that room all night. So, no one could get it. The next morning, the Sister's sent the clock to me before either you or Hattie could retrieve it." Snow spoke decisively.

Thomas leaned forward, elbows on his knees and stared into the cold fireplace. Ash of long dead fires sifted down in a draft.

"John, bring the clock." Snow sat, his face void of expression.

John stepped into the front room and placed the clock on the table between Snow and Thomas. Thomas reached for it, but the obvious   struck him like the chiming of an hour. He pulled his hands back.

"What are you really looking for Thomas? Why did you come here?"

"The Sisters told me she sailed down to St. Mary's with Richard and Carrie. One way or another, I assumed she would get her hands on the money."

Snow spoke softly. "Thomas, Richard told me Hattie went missing from Darberry Farm yesterday. I haven't seen her. When I take your past jealous temper into account, I wouldn't tell you if I had."

Thomas straightened, reproach swept over his face. After a moment, he looked down to his left gathering his thoughts.

"I was not jealous. Hattie was eleven. Ellen Mae sent her to the boatyard with something for James. I was there. When I left, I heard Hattie crying behind the sail loft. A man accosted Hattie on her way to the yard. He grabbed her arm and forced her to kiss him. It was not the first time. She was afraid to tell. Afraid she'd be sent away from her home one more time. I walked her back to the house."

"What else?"

"The man was Dr. Radcliff's nephew. Radcliff said he would send him away. He only took the nephew in as a favor to his sister. The nephew was trouble."

"Did Radcliff send him away?"

"No. I came by two weeks later. Hattie was afraid to leave the house. This time, I didn't bother with Radcliff. When I caught up with the nephew... She was eleven, a little girl." Thomas gave Snow a challenging stare. "I did not intend to kill him. I was drunk."

"Do you know Hattie assists Dr. Radcliff on his general clinic days? Do you know he is training her to be a nurse?"

Thomas nodded. Bitterness like the taste of drifting ashes crossed his darkened face. "Hattie knows something about the day Ellen Mae died. She knows if Ellen Mae was still standing in the kitchen when she left for the boatyard. She knows who arrived back at the Elms from the boat yard first."

After a moment's contemplation, Snow made a decision. "In that case, we need to take a walk to Cawsin Farm." Snow stood. Buddy Jenks moved into view from the center hall. John slipped away.

Chapter 10: A Bend In The Woods

...If th' assassination
Could trammel up the consequence,
and catch
With his surcease, success: that but this
blow
Might be the be-all and end-all –here,
      MACBETH ACT 1, Scene 7
      William Shakespeare

Fingers of shade from front yard oaks reached over the Rest creeping towards Jane's grave among the roses. Snow led the group across the back yard and into the pines. Josiah Jenks and Thomas passed him by as the trail became apparent. Buddy Jenks followed at a distance, retrieved his rifle left by the back porch door, and let the screen door slap shut behind him. As the path through the pines swallowed them all, the screen door shut softly a second time.

Rank odor of decomposing leaves floated lazily up through pine limbs. Cicadas screamed a rising crescendo to the heat of late afternoon. As their shrillness died off, Snow heard Josiah Jenks' astonished shout. Buzzards rose from the base of the king's tree. They lumbered up through darkened forest into waning light of a late afternoon sky. Snow read gruesome surprise on Thomas' face.

The body lay, bloodied from deep ax blows, in brush just behind the tree's base. Face down, Richard Darberry sprawled across a cream-colored shawl. Surveying the body in the underbrush, Snow recalled the clear sharp sounds of Paul's powerful swings while chopping wood. Back down the path, Buddy stood vigilant, rifle ready. Behind him, a shadow retreated towards the Rest.

Josiah warily rolled the body. Clouds of flies and mosquitoes ascended. Scratches played across Richard's face, deep and parallel like the clawing of a wild animal. Dark pools of congealed blood broke open, oozing red. Flies descended with renewed ferocity. Josiah Jenks backed into the path moving towards his brother. Face pale with nausea, Thomas turned towards Snow. John reappeared carrying a rolled boat tarp while keeping a tree between himself and Buddy Jenks. Snow's mind raced through the possibilities and came to a decision.

Snow stared into John's blank expression as he spoke to the Jenks brothers. "My caretaker, John, is behind you. After he wraps Richard's body in a tarp, bring them both to Darberry Farm. Thomas and I are going ahead to find Carrie Darberry."

Josiah spoke up. "Sheriff Thompson needs to see this."

With firm authority, Snow rebuffed Josiah's objection. "We can't leave

Richard out here all night. The sheriff will take my word on what happened here."

Not waiting for any more disagreement, Snow walked briskly back down the path. He avoided looking in the direction of the woodpile behind the summer kitchen. He didn't glance at Jane's grave. The two men marched through the rose garden, around the house, and trotted down the hill. Thomas picked up his pace to a run closer to the wharf. Snow stayed with him, panting as he stepped off the dock into the sloop. Thomas untied the lines. Despite a freshening breeze, he sculled the sloop to the mouth of Snows Run with force. Hoisting sail, he set sail on a reach up the St. Mary's River. After passing Horseshoe Point, they caught sight of Darberry farm. Thomas came up into the wind and tacked over. Lines taut and wind whistling through sails, the sloop took aim at a small dock below the house. Without disturbing the sloop's balance, Thomas stood for a better look. The mainsail shielded him from view. The house interior was dark.

"Front door's open." Thomas dropped the jib and back winded the main sail to stall the sloop. As they slid up to the dock, he wrapped the bowline around a piling. In one motion, he pulled an ancient Civil War era Remington New Model revolver from a wallet strapped under his shirt and stepped onto the dock. The sloop swung around on its line. Snow ducked the boom as it flew through the cockpit. By the time he dropped the main and climbed onto the pier, Thomas had disappeared into the dilapidated farmhouse. Snow scanned the farmyard's shoreline and the woods beyond. Where swamp willows hung out along the shore, Paul's dory bobbed in shallows half hidden. Snow walked toward the house, continuing his scan. Footsteps on creaking boards echoed from the house. Thomas appeared in the doorway.

"Is anyone inside?" Snow hesitated on the bottom step. Thomas shook his head, scanned the farm, and spotted the dory. Snow read the question in Thomas's expression.

"Yes, that's his dory."

"Who's dory?" Thomas' genuine astonishment gave Snow pause. He used several panting breaths to stall his answer.

"I think she's with Paul, my caretaker's son. Paul plays piano..."

"I know who Paul is.", Thomas snapped. He started down the broken, sun-bleached steps and stopped on the bottom. His expression revealed thoughts visibly turned inward, as a cold rain of realization washed through him.

Snow spoke with forced calm. "Is there any sign of Carrie inside?" Thomas took a deep breath and shook his head.

"No. No one inside." They stood together scanning the area. "You stay here." Thomas stepped off the stoop and headed for the woods. Snow didn't waste his breath telling Thomas to wait for the Jenks brothers.

Darkness swallowed Thomas into the trees, as he trotted in the direction of the dory. Darkness surrounded Snow as he entered the house. The floor groaned objections to his cursory search. Through windows in the back, he viewed fallow fields and woods. Through windows at the front, he viewed the pier and St. Mary's River turning pink in the sunset. On the rickety kitchen table, a box of matches sat beside a smoke-darkened oil lamp. His trembling hands fumbled the matches. He raised the glass chimney. Straining to hear sounds beyond the hissing, flickering match flame, Snow lit the lamp. He stepped to the open door and squinted at the sunset flashing off the river. A quiet shadow hovered over the floor behind him. Skirts rustled. A board creaked. A chill crept across Snow's shoulder blade towards his left arm. He turned around a bit at a time.

The lamp's golden orb pressed against darkness, casting shadows across her face. Vapors wavered up from the lamp chimney. Seated in stillness with downcast eyes, she appeared a slumbering dream. "Jane" formed on Snow's lips, but refused to escape. One long, dark tress fell down her shoulder and across the blue linen lapel. She raised her face to reveal her endearing smile from another place and another time. Soft lamplight shimmered, revealing bruises on her throat. A shudder passed through the house.

"William", her soft voice floated through the waning afternoon. "Please come and sit with me, while we wait for Thomas and Carrie." Snow made one hesitant half step towards the apparition. The chill prickled across his shoulder, down his spine, and stayed his step. Something sizable rested under an embroidered linen purse that covered her hands. The open doorway was a half-step behind him, one quick fall backward. At any second, Thomas and Carrie might walk through it. Like partners in a dance, he stepped back , and she raised his missing Colt revolver.

Stumbling, Snow tried distraction. "We came to find Carrie. Richard..." When anger swept across her face, he let the sentence fall to silence. The house groaned and gasped to the beating of his heart. The Colt wavered in her grip.

"Annabelle loved me. Ellen Mae loved me. Richard loved me. Thomas... I will miss them all so much." Sadness swept over her face. The floor creaked loudly. A large, dark hand reached out from shadows and removed the Colt from her grasp. Snow staggered backward with relief onto the porch.

"I love you." Reproach echoed in Paul's declaration of endearment. Pulling his hand to her cheek, she smiled tenderly up at him. Images of Jane's smile floated in Snow's memory. Paul drew Hattie up from the chair, engulfing her in his arms. Pain and pleading emanated from his gaze. "We will go now."

"Thomas will come back soon. He will bring Carrie with him." Hattie's plea had no effect. Paul stuffed the colt and linen purse into a carpetbag. With Hattie's arm in one hand and carpetbag in the other, he brushed past Snow, down the steps, and out to the dock. Snow watched speechless as Paul skillfully guided Thomas' sloop well beyond Horseshoe Point into St. Mary's River.

Thomas appeared gun in hand, his eyes sweeping from Snow to the empty dock and back again. Snow recovered his speech. "They must have come in through back windows when you went into the woods. Have you seen any sign of Carrie?"

"I found Carrie hiding in the woods. She hid when they tied the dory in the shallows."

"Hattie had my Colt. Paul stopped her from shooting me." Snow's words drained hope of Hattie's innocence from Thomas' face. He looked into the dimly lit kitchen, at the table, the chairs, the lamp, and the matches.

"There's a bloody ax in the dory." Thomas's set jaw made his determination clear.

Snow caught a movement in apple trees by the barn. "Did you tell her?"

Thomas shook his head, adding, "I didn't have to. When they showed up without Richard and hid the dory, she feared as much. With my Colt drawn and cocked...Well, it was obvious. Do they have my money?" He turned to stare at the empty dock.

"I s...s..saw them leave." Carrie called from shadows by the barn. "Is it safe?"

"Yes, Mrs. Darberry, we're alone." Snow strode quickly across the yard, and placed a supporting arm around her shoulders, guiding her towards the house. "I'm so sorry. This will be a very hard time for you. We found Richard dead in the woods. The Jenks brothers are bringing him home."

"All my fault." Carrie stumbled, leaning against Snow. "He was trying to protect me from her. Oh, what have I done?"

Snow leaned closely, whispering, "You knew about Abbott? You told Ellen Mae?"

Nodding in misery, Carrie stumbled on between sobs. "Ellen Mae was so angry with me...didn't want to know the truth. I thought she would...turn to Richard. She only wanted to sell land...run away, leave everyone behind. Hattie found a letter from the Pennsylvania Railroad ...they fought."

Two skipjacks slipped around the point and drifted toward the dock under limp sails in a late-in-the-day dying wind. Thomas ran ahead to meet the *Louisa Mae.*

By the time Snow settled Carrie on the porch steps, Thomas' loud demands rang clearly all the way from the dock. Shaking his head vigorously, Snow headed for the *Louisa Mae.*

"Put that away, after you make sure the first chamber is empty." Snow spoke with quiet authority. Thomas looked at his revolver, pursed his lips, and nodded. Snow waited until the revolver was safely holstered.

"Yes, they have the money." His accusing glance at John, who shared the secret of the tunnel, went unnoticed by everyone except Sarah, sitting half-hidden in the skipjack's cabin. "Sarah will stay with Carrie. Josiah and Buddy will help Carrie lay Richard out. She will need them to inform relatives and neighbors. Then, they will find Sheriff Thompson and tell him." After a pause, everyone set about complying.

John, Thomas, and Snow pushed off,

poling the *Louisa Mae* away from the dock, out into the darkening river. Left on the dock, Sarah followed their progress. Her anxious stare, aimed at John, penetrated the gathering, evening mist.

Chapter 11 Legend's End

Every new beginning comes from some other beginnings end.
Seneca the Younger, 4 BC – AD 65

In the river, Snow set the helm on a broad reach along the shore. John trimmed the main sail and jib. Thomas stepped into the cockpit toward the tiller, but Snow blocked his path.

"She's faster on a broad reach. Along the shore, we'll make a straight course through shallows all the way down." Snow's set jaw and intense stare ended the mutiny.

As a cooling wind freshened from behind, the *Louisa Mae*'s chances of catching the sloop improved. The skipjack's flatter bottom and centerboard allowed her a straighter course through shallows past Chancellor Point and St. Indigoes Neck. The three men sailed on, each in the silence of his thoughts.

A low boom, like distant guns, preceded sinister clouds rolling over trees up river. Darkness fell fast ahead of the storm. A white-hot bolt rent the heavens and thundered to ground, leaving a lurid glare over the water. The *Louisa Mae* fished back and forth in fluctuating bursts of wind. Snow gave John the helm without discussion. At Smith Creek, a flash of lightning revealed the sloop's sails ahead past Potter Creek. She was on a beam reach, wind on her port side, headed toward the beach. Water deepened along the shore there, as deep as five feet. Freshening winds were only just reaching farther south at Cornfield Point. Behind them, the St. Mary's River disappeared into a wall of dark torrent punctuated by blinding flashes. Waves frothed up from the river bottom like regiments of soldiers marching from trenches into battle. John brought the *Louisa Mae* around to port on a beam reach and headed into Smith Creek for protection.

"No!" Thomas' outburst and lunge toward the helm rocked the *Louisa Mae*. Snow and John fended him off. "They have my boat and my money. He's letting them get away!"

"Paul'll layover in Hall Pond, before Cornfield Point." John's answer was short as he brought the *Louisa Mae* into Smith Creek. Land between them and the river provided some protection from the storm. Snow took the helm. Thomas dropped anchor, and John dropped the sails. A ghoulish green glow lit up the creek as the *Louisa Mae* shuddered. Lifting with a sensation of a rearing beast, the skipjack rose up and dragged her anchor halfway across the creek. Hail sprayed them like buckshot as a cavalry of heavy rain galloped over the deck. The torrent swallowed them in a wall of darkness.

As fast as it came, the storm spent

itself and the clouds thinned. The *Louisa Mae* sailed out of Smith Creek toward Point Lookout on a changing wind. A silver moon peered between dissipating clouds and revealed shoreline south along the way to Cornfield Point. Straining for a site of the sloop, they sailed past Hall Pond.

Devastation beyond Cornfield Point left them silent for several minutes. Trees of many hundred years lay felled in rows like the first passing of reapers through a ripened wheat field. Other giants, only feet away, stood untouched as silent sentinels. Tree limbs, strewn across Cornfield Harbor, bobbed and ducked dangerously in the muddied waters. Thomas scrambled to the bow, signaling and yelling port or starboard. John followed his direction and sailed a course around the drowned oaks and poplars that lay submerged in their path. Snow scanned the shoreline. John brought *Louisa Mae* around into the wind and tacked back up river. Snow spotted the beached sloop on the second pass.

Leaving the skipjack anchored in shallows, they scrambled over and around trees, through swamp, and along the shoreline. Clay muck sucked at their boots. The sloops upturned bottom was scarcely visible from the river. Now, it seemed a mirage that dissolved into the chaos. They passed by it. Thomas looked back and shouted in amazement at the broken mast tangled in trees behind them. They trudged back and were almost to the wreck before Snow saw an arm and torso wrapped in sails and lines. He turned around attempting to block John's view. Behind him, John stood bent and motionless. Snow walked back and placed his hand on John's trembling shoulder. Thomas looked deep into the tangled wreck of trees and sloop. Stepping back, he waited for them to come.

When John was steadied, Snow guided

him forward through heavy wet clay. Wrapped in rigging and tangled in the arms of a fallen giant oak, Paul lay on his back, eyes dulled. Snow sat John on the broken oak's trunk.

"John, I'm so sorry. He saved my life." Snow blurted out this revelation. John didn't respond, as the dullness transferred from Paul's gaze to his father's.

Thomas pushed into the twisted mass of foliage that embraced the beached sloop. Lifting out a soaked, unopened carpetbag, he raised it in victory. Snow raised his eyebrows in a silent question.

Thomas responded. "No, I didn't see her. Didn't see any sign of her, except this." He opened the bag, and felt through the contents, dropping items onto the dark sand. Hair combs, a mirror, shoes, and clothing dropped one piece at a time. Thomas pushed back into the tangle of boat and tree, searching.

An inconstant moon slid behind sporadic

clouds stealing her light from stretches of shoreline. Snow searched up and down the beach. Somewhere in the direction of Point Lookout Light, impressions of dainty footprints appeared in the silver-lit sand. They went on for several yards before the moon hid them behind her dark shawl. Snow stood as still as if posing for a daguerreotype. When moonlight slid back over the beach, a figure appeared in hailing distance. Snow stumbled forward.

"Hello. I'm William Snow from up St. Mary's River. We are looking for a woman, a survivor of the storm. Have you seen her?" The man, oddly dressed in a loose, wide-lapelled, double-breasted jacket, made no response. As Snow approached, he observed a circular symbol on the jacket's arm. Silvery clouds marched across the moon. The shade of night crept over the beach, obscuring distances.

"My name's Heaney. They drown. The women all drown. Their skirts..." Grief in the man's voice, mournful as wind in trees, held Snow fast in the sand.

"There was only one. We are looking for one." Snow called out to the dark empty landscape. He turned all the way around, looking for the man. Only his own tracks stretched behind him towards the wrecked sloop. Snow plodded back down the shoreline.

"This is useless. I can't see anything." Thomas yelled in frustration, crawling out of the beached sloop's cabin. "We'll sail around to the lighthouse and come back in the morning."

John muttered something under his breath and didn't move.

"Bring us an oil lamp and tarp from *Louisa Mae*. Then help me find wood dry enough to burn. John and I will stay the night." Snow's voice revealed more weariness than determination.

"I be alright by myself. I want to be alone with him." The firmness of John's demand brought Snow up short. Staring at the upturned hull, Snow considered the long night and consequences ahead. Then he nodded and followed Thomas to the skipjack.

Snow gathered the tarp, oil lamp, and matches. To Thomas, he said, "Wait here for me. I'll come back and go on to the Light with you."

When he returned to the *Louisa Mae*, Thomas had lit the masthead lantern. They sailed her into the river and around to Point Lookout Light. Percy Yeatman, son of the keeper William, met them at the pier and helped them tie up.

"Sighted your masthead lantern. Father will be very surprised to see you, Judge Snow. Come up to the house and get dry. Mother will warm you up somethin'." They spent the night in the keeper's front room.

In the morning, Percy returned with them. John and Paul were gone. Footprints dug up the sand around the beached sloop.

Drag marks from the tarp traced a clear path into the swamp. Thomas and Percy followed them to Hall Pond but found nothing. Snow walked down the beach searching for footprints other than his own but found nothing. He returned, sat on the broken oak's trunk, and waited while Thomas searched the sloop's cabin in vain. Percy sailed back to the Light. Thomas and Snow sailed in silence back up the St. Mary's River.

It was a beautiful day for a sail. The river was calm, the wind on the beam soft and easy. There was no hurry about it. Snow sat on the cabin roof in the mainsail's shade, scanning the shoreline.

Thomas sailed back to Darberry farm. Lengthening the legs of *Louisa Mae*'s course, he ran her out in exaggerated zigzags from one bank to the other all the way up river. When they arrived at Darberry farm, Carrie was in the hands of her family. Richard's funeral was the next morning at Saint Francis Xavier Church in Valley Lee. St. Mary's Sheriff Thompson waited on the little dock crowded with boats. Thomas anchored in the cove. Stump rowed himself and Thompson out to the *Louisa Mae*, sat in the small catboat, and listened.

Sheriff Thompson began with, "We spotted the *Louisa Mae* coming up the river. Waited for you. You took long enough." His aggravated greeting was short on ceremony but conveyed a tone of relief. "Constable Stump was over from Solomons for a talk. When the Jenks brothers sailed up to Leonardtown. Josiah Jenks told us some of what happened."

While Thomas recounted the chase and the storm, Snow surveyed the farm. When Thomas told of finding the ax, the sheriff sent a deputy to look for the dory. Snow knew without looking the dory was gone from the shallows. The sheriff made no mention of Sarah. Thomas remarked on his missing money repeatedly. He assumed Hattie had drowned. Snow's thoughts drifted to Old Benjamin and how much Thomas was like his grandfather.

As turmoil and tragedy swirled through the human community, the wide expanse of river settled to indifferent calm. At the cove's edge, trees stared into their own reflection. The river mirrored the sky as puffs of cloud wandered across both worlds. Hidden beneath a mirrored heaven, creek life wandered to view in the *Louisa Mae*'s shadow. A school of spot, fleeing hunting rockfish, flashed silver past the hull and disappeared under a reflected cloud. A crab crawled up the anchor chain, let go and fell into darkness. Truth gave a brief glimpse and darted for cover under a false sky of reflected light.

"With all due respect, Judge Snow, I believe you have something to tell us." A hint of sarcasm in Sherriff Thompson's comment made his jurisdiction clear.

"Sheriff Thompson, it has been a very long day and night, and now another day. Everything that Thomas Coode has told you is true." Snow lowered his exhausted face onto his folded arms. The sheriff's tone abated.

"This man of yours, he has family nearby? Must have family here?"

"There was only the one son. His brothers and cousins all left for the far shore years ago to pick crabs and tomatoes. The son is dead, drowned in the storm. We found him last night. From what we could tell, the father dragged the body into the swamp. We found no sign of other survivors." These few facts fell like leaves into the water and sank into the dark depths of the unsaid.

The sheriff nodded. "Well, maybe that's the hand of God's justice. I'll be taking a search party down to Cornfield Harbor." From his silence, Stump nodded to Snow and rowed Sheriff Thompson back to the dock. Stump stayed for the search and the funeral.

Thomas accompanied Sheriff Thompson and his deputies on their fruitless search and stayed for the funeral. In the end, Thomas asked Carrie to return to the Elms, her home of many decades. She declined. Thomas sailed back to Solomons Island with Constable Stump.

Days passed. Settling into a morning routine, Snow lit a fire for coffee in the summer kitchen. He slowly worked his way through firewood Paul had split that last morning. He baked a poor excuse for beaten biscuits, washed them down with black coffee and finished with a hand-rolled cigarette. He milked the cow, fed chickens, and checked crab traps strung off the pier. Each morning, he wound Old Benjamin's clock. Days went by simply.

One day, Snow searched the crumbling tunnel, not expecting to find anything. He found more earth collapsed from sides and roof, blocking David's hiding place. Returning with a rusted hammer, old boards and square nails from an old barn, he secured access. Hammering hard, he shored up walls, lost track of how many nails, slowed, tired, finally sat and stared.

Another day, he searched John's cabin. Personal items left behind testified to a hasty departure. Contents were scattered across the floor, into the yard; a torn lace curtain hung from a broken window, shards of pottery smashed underfoot scattered across the rough pine board floor. Another searcher had come before of him. Briefly, he wondered if Stump or Thompson would send the searcher to the Eastern Shore, but thought his own duplicity was probably safe.

There were nights his dreams tied up at the dock, floated up the hill and drifted through the walls. Flowing in silk, Jane waited for him to slip a hand around her waist, to gather her to him, her lips parting in silence. He woke taut, tangled in questions, and went in search of his bottle of Melrose Rye.

A night came when he took out the letters and tintype of David found at Cawsin Farm. Looking long into David's weathered face, he pondered the break with honor that sent David into a life of desertion. In the end, what value was there in an honor that separated and haunted them both all those years? For the first time, he focused on the eyes of the child Annabelle. In those eyes, he saw the eyes of Ellen Frances Cawsin and the eyes of Hattie Maud Wells.

All the years lauding the legend of a son fallen in battle lay exposed as a lie. All his years filtered through the guilt of his survival snapped shut like the aperture of a lens. Whether Jane protected him from the truth or the lie, he would never know. He grew tired of it. He willed his anger to be still. Creeping back to his dreams, he pulled Jane to his heart and, with tears, willed her gone. Light lifted his days, and his sleep was deep and long.

One morning, he wandered out to the roses and stood before Jane in silence. Swallows sang their last songs of summer, flitting about the yard. Snow's cold winter of grief melted in the memories of a kiss by a stream. Softly, she called his name. He stood fast. He did not turn. She would not be there. The voice persisted. A white wing touched his arm, morphing to a gloved hand. He turned.

Carrie's concerned smile and gentle voice touched his soul like butterfly wings. Snow gazed into her eyes as if waking from a dream. She prompted him with "I thought you might be alone, so I came... We brought you a basket for supper."

In that moment, he heard the tremble of her voice, glimpsed anxiety in her eyes. Beatrice Overzee's voice came to him, "Mr. Coode needed her to come and she needed somewhere to go." Now, he needed someone to come and, again, Carrie needed somewhere to go. Uncertainty shadowed her face, lurked behind her eyes. He smiled, and the shadow faded.

Snow looked beyond her to a young man in an old double-breasted jacket. Carrie continued with, "This is Will Heaney, a friend of the Jenks brothers. Will was kind enough to bring me here on his way back to Virginia." Snow nodded in recognition. Will nodded back. Without direction, Will moved Carrie's trunk and kitchen supplies up to the Rest from the dock. Life improved.

The day came when Snow found a short handled pruning scythe in a basket of gardening tools on the back porch. He went out to the garden. Paths lay strewn with spent rose petals of late summer. Each breath of wind bathed the grounds in color. Tangles of thorn battled each other and blocked his way. Then he began. He would fulfill his promised to Jane. He would tend the roses himself.

About The Author

Books, books, glorious books have always enriched my life. I grew up in an old country farm house with a fireplace in every room, no closets, and many bookshelves. When I was old enough to drive a tractor in haying season, I always took a book in my lunch pail to read along the shaded edge of wood and field. After morning chores, my favorite activity was a walk to our town library. Surrounded by bookshelves full of Nancy Drew, Kay Tracey, and Trixie Belden novels, I read with a flashlight under the covers late into the night, well past my bedtime. My first employment off the farm was a position as librarian's aid at that same library. After graduating from Bridgewater State College with certifications in elementary education and library science, I spent forty years sharing my love of books with children, those I taught and my own. So, I thought,

L. A. Stewart

"Now is the time!" Retiring to experience books from the other side of the cover, I am delighted with reader reception of the series Snows Maryland Mysteries.

Afterwards the Recipes

Gladys Overzee's Cornmeal Spoon Bread

Beat three eggs and one-fourth cup sugar together. Then add one cup sweet milk and one cup of sour milk in which you have dissolved one teaspoonful soda. Add a teaspoonful of salt and one and one half teaspoons baking powder. Then mix one cup of granulated corn meal and one-third cup flour with this. Put skillet on the range and when it is hot melt in two tablespoons of butter. Turn so that the butter can run up on the sides of the pan. Pour in the corn-cake mixture and add one more cup of sweet milk, but do not stir afterwards. Put this in the oven and bake from twenty to thirty-five minutes. When done, there should be a streak of custard through it. Serve with honey.

Note: In older recipes, fresh whole milk is referred to as sweet milk.

Jane Cawsin Snow's Puff Pastry Shells for Tarts

Wash hands first in very hot and then in very cold water. Measure four double handfuls and one single handful of white flour into a large sifter. Pinch in two measures of baking powder that fill the cupped well of one hand and the same amount of salt. Sift and then sift again. Fill one teacup full of butter and one teacup full of lard. Chill the tea cup of lard in a bowl of ice water until lard is hard. Soak hands in cold water. Rub cold lard into flour mixture until you have a fine paste. Add just enough ice water, say half a teacup, containing a beaten egg white. Mix until a stiff dough. Cut butter in four pieces. Sprinkle pastry board lightly with flour. Care should be taken to use as little flour as possible. More flour will make a tough curst.   Roll paste thin and butter with one piece of butter. Sprinkle lightly with flour and roll it up like a scroll. Fold the ends into middle and roll out again. Repeat three more times until the butter is used up. Roll into a scroll again and place in an earthen bowl. Cover with a damp cloth and place in an icebox or springhouse an hour or more. It should be very cold before making out the crust. Tarts made will be flaky and difficult to cut.

Shells for Tarts

You will need two cookie cutters one large and one small. You may use a glass and a wine glass. The cutters should be dipped in hot water as you cut to make the edges rise when baked. Roll out puff pastry. Cut one large circle. Then cut three more and cut a hole in each with the smaller cutter. Lay these three on the first and bake at once.

L. A. Stewart

Baking Shells
Heating of the oven is important. If you can hold your hand in the oven while counting to twenty, it is correctly heated. Another way to judge heat is to place a small piece of puff paste in oven and bake before baking the whole. The oven should stay heated while tarts are baking. Let bake ten or fifteen minutes until light brown.

Filling Tarts
Let cool and fill with preserves, jams, or marmalade. Filling now preserves the color and flavor of the filling.